Einstein's Shadow Galactic Hauler

T.J. Manrique

Published by Astra Iter Inc, 2022.

This is a work of fiction. Similarities to real people, places, or events are entirely coincidental.

EINSTEIN'S SHADOW GALACTIC HAULER

First edition. August 29, 2022.

ISBN: 979-8986195131

Written by T.J. Manrique.

Also by T.J. Manrique

The Rhea Initiative Project
Einstein's Shadow Galactic Hauler
Zombies That's what happened
Another Boring Day In Space

Watch for more at https://tjmanrique.com/.

Table of Contents

Chapter 1

Tired and stiff, she twisted her torso right, then left, and rotated her head a couple of times.

Fully loaded and en route, all systems nominal, the gargantuan ship hummed along in the darkness of space. The *Einstein's Shadow* Galactic Hauler was a slick, fast, high transport capacity, vastly versatile ship. Those, however, were not the features First Officer Margaret "Maggie" Griffin, called simply First by everyone, was looking forward to enjoying.

First was looking forward to going to the *Einstein's Shadow* fully equipped gym and blowing off steam after a double shift.

Double shifts were not all that rare. They were a typical crew of five, and although the ship was state of the art and practically flew itself, humans were necessary to keep an eye on things. Nobody knew why, but fully automated ships went missing over fifty percent of the time, crewed ships made it to their destination over ninety-nine percent of the time, so all Galactic Haulers were crewed. Small crews, but present nonetheless. Passenger or military ships, all had much larger crew compliments, but that was a different story.

I need to work up a good sweat.

She thought and stretched on the chair, extending her arms over her head as far as they'd go. A puff of breath escaped her lips, as her hands came back down onto the communications console.

Naturally, no signals reached them in flight until they were relatively close to an inhabited planet, and they were in an unpopulated section of their trip. No known inhabited planets anywhere nearby. All the same, communications were constantly monitored. Space regulations, to be followed, whether they made sense or not.

"Hey, First, you almost done, right?"

First smiled at the rough voice coming out of the intercom. Oliver Coulter was the ship's engineer, affectionally referred to as Gears by everyone. He was deeply in love with the ship. Weird and kinky, for sure, but a fact nonetheless. "Yes, Gears, I'm about twenty minutes from being done up here."

"Well, I'm done already. All calibrations and the tuning I had to do. Are you going to the gym? I need a good workout. Maybe a game or two?"

She smiled. Originally, she thought about an intense session with resistance machines, with music blasting in her earbuds, but kicking Gear's butt on racquetball would be satisfying too. "I can play a game or two of racquetball. If you don't mind losing again, that is." She was sure he could sense her teasing smile through the intercom.

"I was thinking of suggesting a game myself. You were just lucky last time."

She shook her head amused, the truth was they were pretty much evenly matched, he won just as many games as she did.

"Guys, I'd like to play too. I need to work up a sweat or I'll rust." The voice breaking through the comm was a deep baritone, which contrasted sharply with their pet name for him.

"Are you done, Noob? You got everything buttoned up already?" Gear's voice was friendly, but stern.

Noob, Jonas Remington, was the newest member of their crew. He joined the crew about five years ago. He was a very capable spaceman, but the lowest person on the table of organizations was always called Noob, which he accepted well enough.

"Yes, mother." First could almost see Noob's eye roll. "Come on guys. This galley work is not my thing. I need to do something physical."

"Fine, fine. First and I will play, when she loses, I'll play you. I'll be tired enough and that'll give you a chance to score a couple of points."

They all laughed at that. First shook her head and leaned into the intercom. "We are all set, then. See you in about half an hour at the gym."

Noob was very athletic. He'd give both of them a run for their money.

She went back to locking up the communication console and going to passive detection only.

"Anything to report, First?" Cap walked in fifteen minutes before his shift started. Captain Thomas Skerrit made it a habit to come in early, but he always left right on time. If he stayed on the bridge, something bad was happening. He rarely stayed at his post late. He had no patience with tardiness. He got rid of crew members for being one minute late.

"Nothing unusual. We are at speed and in the pipe. She's humming like a kitten."

"Kittens don't hum, they purr." He smiled as he read the tablet she handed him.

A blinking yellow light and a high-pitched intermittent signal on the communications control console caught her attention. First approached the console and frowned. "Um, Cap? I'm getting what seems to be a message."

Cap didn't look up from his reading. "Check the sensor array and the antenna. We got a few ghosts yesterday, slight misalignments, nothing more."

First checked the displays. All readings came back nominal. "Cap? I think this one is for real."

"In barren land?" He scratched his cheek, frowning. "See if you can pin-point it."

Five minutes went by and First had a fix on the origin of the signal. "I got it. Pretty garbled, however. I can hardly make anything out of it. It's not static, though, appears to be a coherent signal, just without discernible content."

"A non-align race perhaps? Unknown species communication?"

"No, what I'm getting is standard, human in fact. I receive a few other bands but probably bleed from the main transmission." She frowned and leaned in closer to the equipment. "Cap, listen to this."

She played the signal on the speakers.

"OK, beeps. Repeating. Two sets, a set of two three short ones and one set three long and three short, on a loop perhaps?"

"I recognize the signal, an ancient code. The series of beeps stands for SOS, it's a call for help."

He turned to her, lifting his eyebrows and tilting his head slightly.

"Actually, three short, three long and three short, three sets of three." She marked the beeps with a motion of her hand.

He listened for a few seconds. "Yes, I can hear the pattern now, I detect the small pause between the sets too. Your fascination with ancient culture comes in handy sometimes." His smile took any sting out of the comment.

First went through the long-range sensor data. The origin was a system not far off the pipe. They'd be by it in a couple of days, a little less perhaps. The signal was insistent and continuous. Packed with a lot of nonsensical information, and no matter how much she cleaned it up, she couldn't find anything more specific on it. No ship name, no identification, simply a cry for help. Just a strong signal on the distress band, but little if any discernable information.

She sat back, gave a resigned sigh. "Nothing else, no content. A distress call, for sure, but no details."

Cap, deep in thought, seemed to be considering all alternatives. With a small shake of his head, turned to her.

"Still your shift. What do you want to do?"

She knew Cap meant every word of it. If she decided to go on by and leave it, he'd back her play. If she decided to stop, he'd be behind her decision, too. He was always training her for her own command, his words.

"Regulations notwithstanding, we got to stop. I'd hate to be in trouble this far out here and have someone simply go by."

"Stop where?" asked Gears walking into the bridge.

First turned to Gears. A half-hour or more must have gone by and he probably decided to find out what the hold-up was.

"We've detected a distress signal from a nearby system. We're going to go check it out."

The greedy smirk accentuated Gears' many wrinkles. "Absolutely we should stop." He rubbed his hands. "This far out, it has to be a ship that fell off the pipe. I smell money."

The intercom came to life right at that moment.

"Guys, what's up? I'm here and you guys aren't. Where are you?"

First leaned over and answered the ship-wide with a direct message to the gym. "Still on the bridge, Noob. Get up here."

A few minutes later Noob came in.

First and Cap were at the controls and Gears was at the bridge engineering station.

"OK, what did I miss?"

"We came across a signal and we are stopping to check it out." Cap didn't turn around but kept his attention on the ship controls.

"Yes!" The cheerful exclamation and the air fist bump brought a smile to them all.

"Good of you to approve, Noob. Not that it matters."

"Oh, come on, Gears, don't be a sour puss. You know as well as I do that a wreck this far out means money." He made a bill counting gesture, rubbing his thumb and forefinger.

"I didn't know you were such a mercenary, Noob." First chuckled. Money was in all their minds, she was sure. After all, people stranded in space were always willing to pay handsomely to be taken somewhere they could get home from.

Cap and First concentrated on doing all the pertinent calculations. They would have to get off the pipe, meaning they had to divert from the carefully plotted course for their faster-than-light travel trajectory, create an optimal route to their new intended destination and back, perform all calculations from scratch, and estimate the impact on their fuel and other consumables.

If they found survivors, that would also take a toll on their food supplies and strain the atmospheric regenerators. Small crews had advantages, one was that there was relatively little room needed for food and such. If there were many survivors, they could be in real trouble.

All had to be done before they got off the pipe. FTL was great, but it took time to reach it and to decelerate from it, so something like this was not to be taken lightly.

"Got the numbers." First announced.

"Me too, sending them over." Cap indicated as he sent his calculations to First's screen. He got hers almost at the same time. They each checked the other's calculations and compared them to the computers. If they all agreed, they'd proceed.

"All good, Cap."

"I concur." He looked over at the computer display and some of the sensor readings. "We still have about three hours in the pipe before we get off. Let's plan what we are going to do then."

The work was intense. Gears went back to engineering where Second, Second Officer Julio Motoya was already at his station.

"What's up, Gears?

"We are stopping."

"We are? Why?"

"First caught a distress call. Seems like it's human, but there is a lot of garbage in the signal. Either way, we are checking it out." The huge smile was back on his face.

Second smiled too. "OK. Do we know who or what is sending the signal?"

"No, too garbled. It is enough to be able to tell whatever is sending it is in trouble."

"Do you think it could be a robot ship?"

"Greedy much? We don't know yet. It could be."

Second was working his side of the engines but had a faraway look on his face. "Can you imagine it? Robot ships are always full of goodies. Since they don't have to worry about squashing people, they load those things to the bulkheads with all kinds of machinery, minerals, you know."

"Well, bring your feet back on deck. We still have to get there. If a crew is present, that's that, we'll cash the rescue fee and done. If not, we can claim the salvage or negotiate the rights, but we have to get there first, so, keep your shirt on."

Second started whistling and he had a literal skip on his step when he moved around. Either way, there was money coming, aside from what they were getting for this trip, which was good in itself. So, he was happy.

The claxon sounded through the *Einstein's Shadow*.

"Ready for deceleration." Cap's firm voice announced shipwide.

They carried several hundred thousand cargo containers. They were the center of an immense series of concentric rings. Every twenty-five payload rings, an engine ring interrupted the monotony of the view. The last ring out was also an engine ring. They came off the pipe and started the braking procedures. It still took them two days to come to any reasonable speed to go into the system.

They used the time to make long-range scans, determining the exact location of the origin of the signal and which was the best route to reach the planet. They were all excited. They expected this was going to be a hugely profitable trip.

Chapter 2

Cap walked on the bridge even earlier than usual. It was a sure sign that the way things were progressing made him uncomfortable. First found this odd, since it all seemed to be going according to plan.

"You got a fix yet?" Cap looked over the engine status display at engineering, and wandered around the bridge, checking different screens and readings. A quick, tight nod every time he stopped.

"Yeah. The origin is on the fourth planet. It's on the outer edge of the Goldilocks zone. Still, pretty comfortable. The nights might be a little chilly." She kept her eyes on the different graphs and numbers displayed on the long-range sensor station.

She moved off to the pilot station and corrected the trajectory ever so slightly. Little changes in direction caused by rogue space debris gravitation fields have huge impacts over distance. If they wanted to arrive at the right place, or as close as possible, they must be precise. Satisfied, she went back to sensors.

"OK, I've got prelims here." First didn't look up from her readings. "It's a mud ball. Rocks and sand, the sand is white or close enough to make it appear white from here. The rocks are all light in color. I'm not getting any life signs. Might be too far, or they may be underground."

"Water, though, right?" Cap was still working at the engineering station. The engines had to be used judiciously and with care. A detour such as this was always a dangerous proposition, strict and continuous monitoring, was of paramount importance in order to survive.

"Plenty. Lots of rivers. A couple of sea-size bodies of water, ample polar caps. So, yeah, plenty of water."

"Any signs of life anywhere? On the ocean, perhaps?" The absence of life clearly worried Cap.

"No, none we can detect at this distance. Perhaps they are bottom dwellers."

"Or we are early in the evolutionary history of this planet and they haven't gone on land yet."

"No, I don't think that's it. I've not been able to detect any flora, so there would be nothing to feed on. I think it's barren."

"Well, if the people that crashed are alive, they might be in a bad way," Cap called ship-wide. "Second? Check and fit Alfa for the rescue mission. We'll be taking it down to the planet. Um... Second? Full complement. Two weeks' worth."

"Yes, Sir." Came the immediate answer.

Cap sat on the pilot chair and gazed at the system they were approaching.

"I'm going to place us in a stellar synchronous orbit with the planet." The *Einstein's Shadow* was way too massive in its present configuration to bring into orbit around the planet. They had their own weak gravity field and everything, aside from the internal artificial gravity. Coming close to a planetary body was out of the question.

First looked over her shoulder at Cap.

"What is it? I can tell something is bothering you."

"I'm not sure. We'll have to be a little closer."

As they settled in the chosen orbit around the star, Cap moved over to the sensor suite.

"You got it pinpointed?"

"Yes, got the exact location of the origin of the signal and the details of the wreck. It's big. Really big. Nothing much is working in it, though. The main thing working, the only thing working it seems, is the emergency transmitter. Everything else seems dormant or offline. Some background energy bleeds, but nothing coherent."

"Let's make a more detailed analysis."

They performed an intense analysis, as best they could from a stellarcentric orbit. They discern several ships or rather several ship fragments in the wreck.

"First, how long has Mobula 3 been colonized?"

She searched for the information. While she was looking, though, she recounted in her head their trips to this colony. This was their third mission and it took them three years round trip each time, so she knew it's at least nine years, two round trips, six years total, and one-year time off in between. Three to four months to unload and three to four months to reload, so, roughly, two years, and the year they have been on this trip.

Turns out, according to the computer records, Mobula 3 has been colonized for fifteen years.

"Fifteen years, Cap."

"Something stinks. Bad."

"Why?"

"Some of those wrecks down there are way older, as in thirty or forty years old. There are a couple of fresh ones too. Something doesn't make sense. Let's be careful about this, OK?"

That some wreckage was over thirty years old was great news. That meant it might be from prospecting robot ships. Those were hardly ever used anymore because of their propensity of not getting to the destination due to "Space Specters" in the spacers bar talk mythology, in other words, no one knew why they didn't make it. However, robot ships were always carrying precious cargo. Always. Since there was no crew, they did not have limitations in acceleration and such and were always used for rugged equipment or precious and valuable materials, mineral or metallic. Finding a crashed one always meant a lot of money, and, if no survivors were on hand, they could claim all the salvage rights and execute or negotiate them.

"Here's lunch." Announced Noob, placing the trays with sandwiches and coffee on the auxiliary desktop at the back of the bridge.

He moved over to take a look at First's display. "Wow. Some of those wrecks down on the surface are over forty years old? Really?" The idea of salvage riches illuminated his face. "So, that's a lot of money for sure, right? I mean, those must be robot ships and they always carried valuables in them, right?"

Both Cap and First exchange amused smiles at Noob's exuberance.

"What, you don't want to put in any more time in space? You want to be planet-bound like, now?" First question was only half kidding.

She herself was in the hauling business for the money. Originally, she wanted to travel and see new and exotic locales, but travel times were in years, not weeks or months, and there was little to see en route but empty space. The exotic locales turned out to be very similar, there are only so many ways to colonize an earthlike planet and there are even fewer ways to terraform one. After the first few, they all seem alike and they were, after all, just breaks in the monotony of shipboard routine.

Most ports of call were frontier planets that needed and welcomed what they brought; they needed all the cargo they supplied them with for survival in a hostile environment. The crew got well paid and they had nothing but money, no property, nothing beyond what they carried onto the ship every trip. However, she had her eye on a villa, in a small town, in a well-developed and modern rimward world, overlooking an ocean. She could be living a life of leisure there, away from everyone.

Space haulers as a rule worked thirty-five to forty years and then retired planet-side. Some chose to purchase a ship and travel as owner-on-board, making even more money. But what good was money if you never spend it? She didn't think that'd be for her, thank you very much. She knew Cap was, in fact, the owner of the *Einstein's Shadow*, he had been at this for what seemed to be a lifetime.

Noob's face colored a deep crimson, "Oh, come on First. You know I like the ship. And I like you guys. It's just that, you know, money is money." His rugged features a bemused worry mask.

Cap's laugh was explosive. "Well, that's some really deep psychological insight all right." He sobered up and continued. "Don't sweat it, Noob. It'll either be a profitable side trip, or it won't. Either way, the main reason for us should be checking to make sure no survivors are trapped down on that mudball."

First nodded in agreement. "Tell you what, why don't you go down to the Shuttle Bay and place a couple of buoys in Alfa? Make one a straight salvage rights signal and one, crew rescued, recovery pending. That'll cover all the alternatives, I think." She noticed Cap's expression was serious. "Anything else he should get, Cap?"

"No. You covered pretty much everything. You good, up here?"

"Sure. I got it. I just have to transfer some information into Alfa's computer and we'll be ready to rock."

"OK. No rush. I'm going to the gun locker. I want to go in with protection. Second outfitted Alfa with the basic needs, but I think we may need something in the way of defense. Noob, you are with me. We'll get the buoys on the way."

They walked off the bridge, leaving First to consider Cap's actions. What did he see that she didn't? Why did he want to go in armed? She gave her head a shake. He had his reasons and rank did have its privileges.

Cap always insisted they practice with weapons when on leave. At least once a week ideally, but no less than twice a month, he paid for everything, the weapons, and the ammo. If you wanted to go shooting at other times, it was on you. They had experience with every conceivable weapon, short of heavy artillery. The crew took it all in stride, a fun activity with your shipmates.

On the ship, the same schedule was maintained, but in virtual reality ranges.

I guess all that practice is going to come in handy.

She couldn't see how it would, though, given that there were no life signs on the planet. However Cap was very well-liked not just because of his personality, he earned their respect many times over. His experience was vast and undeniable. They had never been on a bad trip. Ever. So, if he said take it easy, and go in armed, they did so. Simple as that.

THEY PARKED THE RIG safely in a star synchronous orbit, in the shadow of the target planet. Alfa, the biggest of the three shuttles on board, was fully equipped, fueled, and ready to launch. Alfa was practically a ship all by itself. Capable of interstellar travel, they used it sometimes for side hustles.

Cap turned to them as they boarded Alfa. "Here we go. I want you to be fully battle-ready. Tactical vests, blasters, first aid kits, the works." Cap's full military-grade weapons complement was not a secret on board, they all knew about it. Curious, to the crew, but no one openly asked questions on the why or how, although they all talked about it.

Einstein's Shadow had a complement of five crewmembers. It could be run easily by three when in the pipe, and by two when parked. Leaving Gears and Second on board, Cap, First, and Noob crewed the shuttle going down to the planet.

“Let's make three full planetary orbits before we set down. Let's start with a high orbit, First, slow and easy, I want detailed readings of the whole planet.”

First complied. It was evident to her that Cap perceived the situation to be dangerous. She didn't see it, which worried her. A lot. What could he see that eluded her?

Cap studied the readings of the wreck from planetary orbit, taking full advantage of the three quick passes at different altitudes. This close, their readings were much more detailed.

"OK. Let's take her down. First, see that hill, tall dune, whatever, between us and the wreck?"

"Yes, Cap."

"Set us down on the far side from the wreck, let's keep it between Alfa and the site."

"Why the precautions?" Noob asked.

"If there are survivors, they will be waiting whether we park here or right next to them, but I'd rather approach slow and easy. We've gotten a single human hit on sensors, one guy, at most. No sense in giving them something to shoot at, if there are more camouflaged in the wreck. If there are survivors and they need help, First will bring the shuttle closer. If we see there's trouble, First will rescue us. Simple." *It never is, but I can always hope.* Thought Cap.

First performed a textbook-perfect landing. Cap and Noob disembarked, they all put on full combat gear, including First, although as the best shuttle pilot of the three, she stayed on Alfa.

As soon as the all-terrain vehicle left the ramp, it came up, sealing Alpha again. They headed to the wreck carefully. Slow and easy.

As they move off, First remained in the shuttle and started to worry about them. They were armed, but they didn't know anything about what they may find.

The sensor alert demanded First attention. A life form was coming up from a cliff face east of the landing zone. Apparently out of the stream at the bottom of it.

"Cap, I've got a visitor. You want to abort and come back?"

Cap considered the situation, as he looked back at Alfa and forwards in the direction of the wreck.

"Negative, First. We'll go all the way to the wreck, if you determine the incoming are hostile, shoot them, take off and come and pick us up."

"Copy that. Will keep you apprised."

First unlocked weapons controls and swiveled the outside guns. The incoming was at the outer edge of the weapon's lateral field of fire. Coincidence? Strategic approach? She simply didn't know.

As the bogey approached, she confirmed the initial reading, the life form was human, undernourished, and a little dehydrated.

The approaching man was clearly in First sight. Ragged and disheveled, now, the person approached desperately signaling with some rag as a flag. The waving was desperate but weak.

She let him approach without leaving the cockpit. She had her eyes on the sensors as well as the castaway. She realized the person was screaming something, so she activated the outside comm.

"Call them back! Quick! It's a trap." He stumbled a couple more steps and collapsed face forward on the floor.

"Cap. It's a human, he's screaming about getting you guys back. He says it's a trap. He just fell and is not moving." She gave her hands a nervous rub on her pants to dry the sweat, her heart racing, but her voice was calm and steady.

"Copy that. We are turning around now." Cap turned the vehicle around and headed back. "Noob, man the gun."

Noob unbuckled, jumped out of his seat, and took his position on a swivel gun mounted on the rear of the vehicle. He strapped himself in and took the safety off, every surface freezing cold even though they had been out in the planet's atmosphere for very little time.

Cap was driving fast and screamed over the rushing cold air back at Noob. "Hold your fire until fired upon, we don't know the score yet and we'll make it back to the shuttle easily. It's not far, we don't want to take sides in a fight we know nothing about."

"Got you, Cap." Noob didn't put the safety back on, he wanted to be ready to fire, if necessary.

First kept her attention divided between the fallen castaway and the returning vehicle. It seemed to crawl over the fine white sand, although the impressive plum of dust growing behind them indicated it was coming back fast. She readied the shuttle for departure without taking her eyes off the sensors.

Cap slowed the vehicle down as they approached the castaway.

"Noob, be ready to pick that guy up. Don't linger and if he puts up a fight or attacks in any way, shoot him and leave him."

"Yes, Sir." Noob unbuckled and gripped the blaster on his belt to activate it.

The vehicle came to a violent stop, kicking up a dense cloud of dust, Noob had a fix on the body on the floor, now obscured by all the dust. He pulled the guy up on the passenger seat, closed the seatbelt on him, and fell in the gun emplacement as Cap started the vehicle back up, at speed in seconds.

"I've got Alfa ready to go, Cap." She called out in the ship-wide intercom as soon as she saw the vehicle clear the hatch. She hit the switch and the heavy door started to close quickly.

"Hang on, First. We have seen nothing threatening yet. What do the sensors show?"

"Nothing, all clear." She ran another long-range sweep, but the results did not change.

Cap ran into the cockpit. "Let's take a more detailed look."

They spent a few minutes running all the scans they could think of, but, aside from the emergency signal, there was nothing to find.

"We could go up to orbit and keep an eye out, while we sort this out." First was still keeping an eye on the sensor readings.

Cap sat back on the pilot chair and let out a long breath. "There is a lot we don't know. We have no idea who our friend back there is, or why he thinks this is a trap. The guy right now is a mystery, nothing more. We need some more intelligence before we leave." He scratched his cheek. "All clear? No contacts?"

"Nothing. This is a deserted mudball. Quiet as a grave." As soon as the words were out, she regretted her choice of expression.

Cap, however, let out a loud chuckle. "I can tell where your mind is at."

He shook his head and stood up, clearly coming to a decision.

"Let's stay the night." His voice firm, his decision made. "Call the rig and tell them everything that happened. Let's keep a sensor feed going both ways, OK?"

"You got it, Sir." First got to work, staying the night might be a good idea. Might also be an unnecessary risk. Hoping her earlier comment was not prophetic and this planet did not become their grave, she sighed and decided to trust Cap's judgment.

NOOB WAS ABOUT TO CHECK on the castaway when the smell of breakfast woke him.

"I'm thirsty." The emaciated man looked with a little apprehension at Noob. The castaway seemed lost and frail. The utilitarian emergency disposable coveralls were never flattering. On anyone. They had gotten most of the grime off him, but there had been no time, and no one had the inclination, of bathing the unconscious man. Noob was a big man and used to people being intimidated by his size.

"We figured you would be. Here." He handed the castaway a bottle of ice-cold juice.

The castaway drank all the juice in a single go. Immediately putting the bottle down, squeezed his eyes shut, pinched the bridge of his nose, and grimaced.

Noob chuckled. "You got brain freeze. I mean, you are a little dehydrated and all, but take it easy." He stood up and extended a hand to the castaway. "Come on, Cap would like to talk to you."

The castaway looked at the hand, sat up, and tried to get out of the cot, only to fall back on it. He shook his head a little and took the offered hand. Noob pulled him up with no effort at all.

As they walked into the galley, the castaway leaning heavily on Noob, Cap, and First turned towards them.

"It's so good to be among humans again. The aliens are dangerous. It's good to be away." He sat and served himself a glass of water from a pitcher on the table and drank the water until the glass was empty. He smiled at all of them. "Wow, this must be a large vessel, I can't tell the gravity is artificial."

Cap crossed his arms and leaned back on the chair. "We are still on the planet."

The blood drained from the castaway's face. He trembled uncontrollably.

"We must leave, we must leave right now. If you give them a chance, they'll sabotage your ship and we'll be marooned again. I can't stay here any longer. I'd die." The castaway buried his face in his hands as his shoulders shook in time with loud desperate sobs.

First looked around, they were all shocked at the strong reaction from the man. He may be delusional. Or not. If he was not, then they were in danger. Mortal danger.

Chapter 3

"We have nothing showing on sensors. Near or far. What about you, Second, anything on your sensors?" First asked on comms, the position of *Einsten's Shadow's* giving it the high ground advantage.

"Nothing, First. I'm not reading any biologicals, no life signs. Just you guys."

Cap leaned back on the pilot's chair. "He seems legit. He is scared out of his mind, he's not faking."

"But of what? We can't find anything." First said through tightly clenched teeth and a low hurried voice.

Cap shook his head and called out ship-wide, "Noob, bring our guest up here."

"Coming, Sir."

The castaway, Benedict Malraux, came on the bridge and headed straight for Cap.

"You have to listen to me. You have to. We are in imminent danger." His trembling hands and chin punctuated each word, his wild eyes going from one face to the next, settling eventually on Caps. "Please, let's take off, please. We need to leave this place. I can't, I just can't go through it all again. I can't." He collapsed on a chair; his head fell forward and thick tears escaped between his fingers. His heaving back keeping time with his sobs, a pathetic spectacle.

"Could the aliens be so different they don't register in our sensors?" Gears asked through the communicator.

"Hey, What kind of aliens?" Noob asked the castaway, none too gently.

Cap looked over at Noob, but saw he was just trying to have the man snap out of it.

The red-rimmed eyes shyly peeked over the hands, "They are small, a little smaller than us, hairy little beasts, bipedal and two arms, their ears are like a lynxes', on top of their head ..." He sobbed again and covered his face in his hands. Muffled, they could hear his voice, pleading. "Please, let's go, please."

"OK, democracy time. What do you guys think?" Cap asked out loud, the *Einstein's Shadow* still on the open communicator.

Noob was the first to answer. "We are right here, guys, let's just go over, on the shuttle, place the buoy and blast off this rock. Nice, quick, and clean." He straightened up and crossed his arms.

First jumped in next. "Actually, I don't see why not. I can maneuver the Alfa right up next to the wreck, you can have the buoy ready and rush out and back in. Fifteen minutes and we are gone. I mean, we can't find any signs of these ... these ... aliens or whatever."

Gears' rough voice came over the speakers. "I don't see it. I think it'd be best for you guys to head back here and get going to Mobula 3. We have Ben. He can witness our salvage claim. I don't see any reason we should take any risks. Besides, we deployed star cartography drones, Stellar Cartography pays for details of unknown systems, they'll go nuts for charts of this system, it's so far out of the way. If aliens are hiding somewhere, they may remove the buoy anyway, so it's a losing proposition all around. I'm just saying."

"What do you think, Second?" Cap asked casually.

"Cap, I'd like you guys back. The trip, this trip, we are getting good money. Benny, he will probably be good for a couple of bucks, you know for rescue fees. At least for the fuel, even if he doesn't pay it himself, we can collect at least some from the Colonial Government, you know, so I say let's move out. It's prudent. If we can claim salvage rights, that'd be a bonus. Also, like Gears here just said, if the aliens, if there are aliens, take the buoy out, it's a useless exercise. I'm just saying, let's get going, I'd rather have you all back."

Benedict looked from one crew to the other and at the speaker on the roof. "Please, don't call me Benny. Just Ben." His voice trembling.

Cap reclined on the pilot seat, thinking hard. It came down to him. It would anyway, this was not, in fact, a democracy, but he always wanted to be sure the crew followed him because they believed it was the right move, not because he ordered it. He liked to listen to everyone before making up his mind. A deep sigh escaped his lips.

"Well, I'm sorry Gears. Second. We are going to the wreck, a quick in and out, and place the buoy."

"You are the captain." Gears' voice was soft, no argument from him.

"What made up your mind? I know money is not the deciding factor." First asked, intrigued. Cap did very well, so any money involved here was the icing on the cake, not the main course.

"It's simple really. We don't know anything about our guest here." He gestured towards Benedict with his head. "He may be telling the truth, although we have seen nothing at all that supports his story, but he may not. Taking a quick look at the wreck will give us a clearer idea of what's going on."

"What are you saying?" Exploded Benedict. "That I'm ... what? A liar? You think I'm making this up?" He was up and panting hard, his fists balled by his sides, his whole-body trembling. "I've been here I don't know how long, barely surviving, I'm telling you if you stay, we" he paused and made an all-encompassing gesture with his hand, "we are all going to die."

"The problem is that we can't detect anything, no aliens. Where is your ship? Where did it crash?" Cap sat forward and rested his elbows on his knees, interlacing his fingers.

"It didn't crash, we came down to check on the emergency distress signal, same as you." Benedict paused for a moment to wipe the sweat from his forehead with his forearm. "We were on a business trip to Mobula 3, we detected a signal, we went up to the wreck, we were exploring it when they... when they ..." he had been raising his voice on the last sentence, finally he broke. He went up to Cap and grabbed him by the lapels. "You have to get us out. Get us out now. Now."

Noob was on him in an instant and secured him from behind. "What do you want me to do with him, Cap? Should I put him out of the shuttle?" The last statement was like a tranquilizer dart. Benedict ceased his struggles and immediately became compliant.

"No, please, don't, please, I couldn't take any more time outside. Please." His breathing was quick and ragged. His eyes, wide open, they saw white all around his irises.

"Let him go, Noob. OK, Ben. Sit in that chair and don't interfere. Let's get this done quickly."

Noob stayed at a station close to Benedict. Cap noticed it and approved, without saying a word, he didn't think Benedict would try anything, but better safe than sorry.

"Anything else? Can you clean up the signal now that we are this close and you've had time to work on it?" Cap was looking at different sensor sweeps. All negative.

"No. I can't clean it up. The signal is strong but has a lot of bleed into other bands, and whatever the content is, it's very garbled. I can't clean it up."

"That's because this is a trap. A trap. The signal is like that on purpose. We were able to locate the transmitters before they attacked us. There are several in the wreck, the only thing that is not mangled beyond recognition. There are some human transmitters and several from different known races. Also, a couple we could not make out, new species, we guessed. Before we could make a more in-depth examination, we were attacked. We fought them off and returned to the ship, we even took off, we gained a little elevation, a few meters, perhaps, no more than that. They brought it down. They incapacitated our ship. Then they boarded us and ... and ..." He finished with a sigh and his shoulders slumped forward.

"Gears? Anything at all from up where you are? Any movement? No matter how far away." Cap asked the communicator.

"Nothing, Cap. Nothing at all, just the emergency signal."

Cap tapped a stylus he had in his hand several times on the console in front of him. He straightened up. "Ok, let's do this, quick and by the numbers. I don't know if these aliens are real and around, but we are going to behave as if they are. Quick in and out. Noob, set up the crew rescued/salvage pending buoy. First, jump us to the wreck, not too close, a short walk away. I'll keep an eye on the wreck, at the smallest sign of activity of any kind, we abort and go back to the *Einstein's Shadow*. All clear? Let's go."

FIRST BROUGHT THE SHUTTLE up to speed and the quick hop to the wreck was over in less than five minutes. Cap and Noob were down by the outer hatch and ready to go. The landing, perfect.

"On station. Go."

"Copy, First. Keep the engines warm." Cap's voice came strongly over the sounds of the hatch cycling. She followed all the processes on her readouts.

"I hope you are right. Please, please, tell them to hurry." Ben sat in the chair close to the back, but she knew he could still hear everything and peek at some of the readouts.

"They'll be fine. We have a lot of experience." First smile was shallow. She was deeply worried. She kept a wary eye on Ben, it was not a matter of not trusting the guy, it was a matter of not knowing anything about him, just as Cap said. Trust did not come easy for First. She'd been burned before.

Cap and Noob made it to the wreck with no incidents. Noob fixed the buoy onto the wreck, while Cap went inside the structure.

"OK, I'm in. Abandoned, no doubt about it." Cap's voice came through loud and clear. His panting was the only evidence he was exploring the wreck quickly. The video signal showed panels of different technologies. The dark shadows in the passages were broken every so often by shafts of light coming through tears in the fuselage.

"There are several different structures here. Haphazardly put together in a crude attempt to make it look like a single vessel from far away. All kinds of remnants of technology, all from different periods, but everything around this side has been heavily vandalized. Nothing seems even remotely able to be repaired. There is a lot here, though, I can identify some valuable scrap metal sections. There is some tech, too, but not in working order for sure. We could make some money here after all. All on salvage, but maybe worth the trip. There is a section here that looks pretty new, must be Ben's ship. It's completely gutted though."

"Buoy active. Do you read it, First?" Noob's baritone broke in.

"Loud and clear. What about you, Second? Reading it fine?"

"Five by Five, got it. We read it perfectly from here." Second swiftly answered.

"Noob, I'm toward the prow of the wreck, you search aft. Quickly, give it a few minutes, and then let's get out of here. The place is giving me the creeps, and not just because of Ben's stories. This place has been looted. Systematically and with intent. All functioning tech is out, but I can tell a lot of salvageable materials are still here. I found heaps of robot parts back here too. Something doesn't make sense."

"Copy that, Cap. Going aft, quickly, and then out." Came the panting response.

First kept her eyes on the sensor console, stealing a glance every so often at the images coming in from inside the wreck. Still, everything was quiet. Nothing registering anywhere. She also kept a wary eye on Ben, he had done nothing else and was still wringing his hands and fidgeting nervously on the chair in the back. His breathing was quick, the raspy breaths audible to her. She was becoming more apprehensive as time went by, her breathing rapid, and her pulse raced.

"OK, that's time. Let's go back." Cap's voice was still calm, although the panting was now more pronounced.

"On my way back. This place is trashed, whoever came on board took everything off the bulkheads. I mean, most doors are gone, there are two strong rooms, open, the whole thing is—"

"Talk about it on board. Just get back here fast." First broke in. Her heart raced and she was starting to pant too, cold sweat dripping down her temples.

"On my way. Keep your pants on." A slight chuckle was discernable among Noob's heavy breathing. First hoped he was quick. Something was wrong, she didn't know what, or if it all was a mind game from listening to Benedict, but her stomach was tight and she was gritting her teeth in anticipation.

"I'm out, walking to Alfa."

"I see you Cap. I'd rather you run." First was quick to point out.

"I will as soon as Noob's with me." Cap was walking back but looking over his shoulder often and then in every other direction, his head on a swivel.

Ben walked up to First. "Please, tell them to hurry. Please."

"They are on their way; it'll all be over in less than five minutes."

"I hope you are right." Ben's whispered comment may not have even been intended for her.

Noob dashed out of the wreck and started running to catch up with Cap, then both ran all out to reach Alfa.

First had timed the hatch coming fully opened with their arrival, and they both ran in and slapped the hatch closed. They kept moving fast up to the bridge,

"Let's go. Let's get off the planet." Cap belted himself in the pilot's station.

"Finally." Ben was back on his chair and belted in, wringing his hands, trembling all over.

Noob strapped himself in. "Ready."

First was ready and kept scanning the area. "Good to go."

The ship trembled a little as it took off. It started gaining altitude and a collective sigh of relief escaped everyone's mouth.

A smiling Ben rubbed his face with both hands. "Well, I hope you are all happy, you took years off my life with the little stunt back on the surface. I mean, I could have told you that—"

"Shit! Activity. I've got an energy spike. Over to the east relative. On one of the rock formations." First took a quick swipe to dry the sweat rolling down her forehead. "What do you see, Gears?"

"Got it. We see it. It's a camouflaged hatch of some sort ... Damn. Get ready to take fire, two missiles underway. Unknown configuration."

"Got them. I see them." Cap was already taking evasive action.

The sad whimpering from Ben at the back was unintelligible, the only word occasionally clear was "please".

"Deploying Electronic Counter Measures." Noob baritone was calm, but his movements had all the urgency the case required. "Negative, no effect. Damn. I can't break the lock."

"That there is a big facility underground." First voice was firm, it showed none of the fear freezing her guts. "Now that the hatch is open, I can detect all kinds of activity. I don't have a headcount, but I detect many life forms down in that underground cave. Novel, we don't know these folks."

"We don't want to meet them either," Cap grunted as he took different evasive actions. "Let's try and get away from them, shall we?"

At that moment, the heavy impact on the rear of the shuttle rocked them in their seats.

"They got us. Perfect hit." Noob's frustrated expression was mirrored by them all.

"Lost engine exhaust, I have to land." Cap was already making the pertinent adjustments, although they had gained a little altitude, he did not want to crash, that would be a disaster.

"No more incoming. What a hell was that?" First frustration and bewilderment were evident in her voice.

A wailing cry ripped out from Ben. "Please, please, no. I don't want to go back to the planet. I'll die. Please." He moaned.

"I'm coming down as far as I can from the attacking rock formation. As close as I can to the wreck, maybe we can take shelter inside if we need to." Cap was wrestling the controls.

"Cap, put this crate on the ground, we need to turn those engines off. The sooner the better." First eyes followed the increasing temperature gauge. The engines, with their exhaust blocked, were overheating. Quickly going into the danger zone. The heat could cause irreversible damage or an explosion. Neither was a palatable option.

"Almost there, almost." Cap's jaw muscles got a good workout, although flying Alfa required no great physical strength, at this time, he was as tense as a violin string. The wounded ship rebellious to his every command.

"Down. Shutting engines now." Cap exclaimed as he hit several switches and controls in quick succession.

"We are OK, we are down. No damage to the engines."

"OK? OK? You think we are OK? Are you insane or just stupid? We are as good as dead!" Ben was screaming now, his voice falling into falsetto notes as he lost control.

Noob was by his side in a flash and grabbed him by the throat in a vice-like grip of his big hand. "You can calm down or I can put you down. No difference to me." What made the threat credible was the absolute matter-of-fact way Noob delivered it. No animosity, no rush. Calm and cold. First had seen Noob take down bigger guys than Ben. He was literally a gentle giant but was also absolutely right. They needed to concentrate.

Ben's shiver was visible even from where she was. His hands were tight around Noob's wrist, but it was like grabbing a bundle of steel cords. "OK, OK, I'm calm. I'm calm. I'm sorry."

After a pause. Noob let him go. "Behave." The same calm, sure tone of voice. Ben meekly sat a little further back on the chair and rubbed his bruised neck.

"Now what?" Asked a profoundly troubled First.

"Now we see just how dangerous these aliens really are." Cap's calm answer did not take away from the fact that they were in trouble. Very bad trouble.

An icy hand seemed to close around First's stomach with each word.

Chapter 4

"What the hell did they hit us with?" Noob wondered out loud. First wondered about that, too.

"They did that to us, too." Ben's shaky, meek voice came from behind them. "Some sort of polymer. It adheres to the hottest part of the ship, the exhaust. The material obstructs the outer openings. You overheat quickly. It's very effective. We chipped some of it away before they attacked us. Not enough, we didn't do it fast enough." His voice trailed off at the end, barely audible, but the bitterness in his voice was quite evident.

"It would have been useful for you to tell the story before it happened to us, you fool." Noob's voice thundered on the bridge. His attention was still on the console in front of him, his hands flying over the controls.

"We are cooling down, slowly but we are cooling down. We may want to try what he suggests, go out and, what did you say? Chip the gunk off? I'm not detecting further movement from the aliens." First's attention was divided evenly between the sensor suite and the engineering section.

"You weren't listening to me. I would have told you. I told you we needed to leave, I told you, you would not listen." Ben's voice trembled.

"Enough, this is pointless." Cap turned to his console and took in the readings. "Let's figure out what repairs need to be made. Check everything out. Make sure that ... stuff outside is simply blocking the exhaust, make sure is not corroding the ports or something."

First hadn't thought of that. The substance could have more than one function. She went back to her readings to make sure all was in order, while Ben's mumbled monotone droned on at the back of the bridge.

"I told you, didn't I? I told you this could happen to you. We were lured by the wreck too, and we placed our buoy to claim it. The aliens eventually removed it; they took the buoy with them too. They attacked us, a numerous group of the little hairy savages, and took our ship. The bits they did not need or want, they left in the pile, there at the wreck, the rest of the tech they took with them."

He was not talking to anyone in particular, the feverish activity on the bridge, was lost on him completely. "I didn't know where they took everything, not then. They simply took everything useful away. I was hiding and survived. My companions were all captured and I couldn't do anything. We all fought, but the alien's armor is impervious to small firearms and we did not have blasters. I ran away and hid, in some rocks, thinking I might survive." Ben's hands were limp on his lap, his head fell forward as if the effort of remembering was too much for him. First thought he was done with his tale, she was only half-listening anyway. The readouts and alternative courses of action demanded her full attention.

Ben was quiet for a few moments. Then, his voice stronger, but still choked, was easy enough to hear, "The aliens are coming anytime, you really should prepare to defend yourselves." He slumped forward once more and remained quiet.

"All clear here. The stuff they hit us with has hardened somewhat, but it's not rock solid, it can be removed fairly easily, I think. No corrosion, or any other overt signs of damage to the ship, seems pretty inert actually." The low temperature of the planet's atmosphere helped cool down the material, surely.

Noob mimicked First's matter of facts tone as he delivered his report. "I can't detect any movement anywhere. The open hatch allows for sensor readings inside. At least to a point. There are a lot of them, but I don't have a count either. I ... I don't register any humans. Sorry, Ben."

Ben lifted his head slowly, to look at Noob. "I ... I sort of expected that."

"So, Cap, what do we do?" First wanted to do something. They could not stay immobile, helpless, waiting.

"Time to go out, set up a perimeter, and clear the exhausts, that has to be our priority at this time. Also, I want everyone geared up. Full combat compliment, let's make sure we don't get caught with our trousers down again. I think it's time to break out a few party favors from storage, OK?"

"Copy." Both Noob and First answered immediately.

"Um, Cap? What about Ben? Do we outfit him too?" Noob's voice made it clear that he didn't think it was a sensible idea.

Cap looked long and hard at Ben for a few seconds. "Do you know your way around a blaster, mister?"

"I know enough, and I'm sure as hell not facing those ... those ... things with nothing in my hand again. Just give me something effective to fight with and I'm with you." Some strength worked itself back into his voice. First sighed inwardly, that was a good sign, she didn't want to have an unarmed person hiding and maybe hindering their efforts to defend Alfa.

First maned Alfa's weapons. The shuttle had exterior cannons and some other surprises not usually found on civilian shuttles.

First heard Cap's steady voice as they made their way down the ramp.

"Slow and easy. We don't want any more surprises."

"Clear scope, Cap." First kept her attention on the sensors but also looked out every so often. They were in a precarious situation, no precaution was too much.

"The sand is fine enough, this will be quick." Noob commented on comms, while Cap made a circuit around Alfa, looking everywhere.

"Cap, all due respect, it'll go faster if both of you plant those things in the ground."

"No, Noob, leave those, I'll finish. Clear the exhausts."

"On it."

Soon, Cap finished the defense perimeter and they both went to work on the polymer attached to the ship. It came off readily enough, but the pungent chemical odor made them have to take turns chipping it away. They cleared about half of it off and needed a break, it was late enough in the day that eating dinner sounded like a fine idea. They went back on board.

"Any movement from our friends?" Cap asked as he walked on the bridge.

"No, they are milling around down in alien town, but they have not come out, not yet, at least. Phew, that's some strong stench." First fanned the air in front of her face, smiling to take the sting her words may have.

"Nasty. We can't work on the stuff for more than a few minutes before we have to walk away to get some air." Noob told her as he walked over to engineering. He took a look at some readouts and tested the engine's response. "We can start them, they'll overheat, but they can give us fifteen, maybe twenty minutes of flight time right now. We couldn't make orbit, but ..." He shook his head thinking hard.

"No, let's eat, rest and go back out. We'll finish tonight and go up as soon as we can. We need off this rock." Cap headed towards the galley.

"We could go back out and finish up, Cap, we don't have that much more to go, and ..." Noob shrugged.

Cap paused at the entrance of the bridge. "No, Noob, we are tired and we need to eat. We need to be ready for anything, if we are attacked and exhausted, we might not survive. I'd rather we ate, rested a little, and went back out."

"Sir." Noob's succinct answer was followed by his intense work on the console in front of him. He obeyed, but his body was hunched and tense.

Cap was gone, down the passageway, to the galley.

"He's the captain, Noob. We trust him. He knows what he is doing." First started in a conciliatory tone of voice.

"I'm not that tired, I could keep going for a while, I ..." He shook his head and shrugged.

"You'd tire yourself out and if there's a fight coming, I want you sharp and able to crack skulls. Come on, let's get this done, OK?"

Noob nodded, took a last lingering look at the engine sensor readings, and followed her to the galley.

First routed the exterior sensor readings to a display on the galley. She gave the *Einstein's Shadow* a call. "You guys comfy up there?"

"A lot better than you down dirt-side, First." Gears chuckled.

"Hilarious. A regular comedian. Listen, I'm putting you through to the galley, we are eating and–"

"All at the same time? Who's manning the sensor station?" Gears interrupted her, worry evident in his question.

"You are. I just fed the sensor output to the galley, but I want you guys to keep an eye on our immediate area too. I'll leave an open channel, we can chat, to keep you awake, old man."

"Old man. I get no respect."

"No more than you deserve is all I'm going to say on the subject. You are patched to the galley, talk to you from here."

SITTING AROUND THE table and keeping a wary eye on the sensor readings, they indulged in a quick, power bars meal with lots of fruit juice.

"This is a good time for you to tell us more about your time on the planet, Ben. Tell us what happened after the aliens attacked your ship. How did you escape?" Cap asked around a mouthful of power bar. He was aware that they were taking their time, and that it might be putting them in further danger, but they needed as much information as they could gather. Furthermore, he had been in fights before, he didn't know how long their fight would be if it came to that, but he wanted them fed, rested, and ready.

Ben was ravenously eating his bars, took a long swig of juice, and licked his lips. "We went out to try to chip that stuff off the ship. It was late. A lot later than now, planet time. They came at night. You need to be careful and alert. Please, listen to me this time, these aliens like to attack at night. You will not see them coming. We didn't."

First swallowed the last of her bars. "Ben, what did you do? How did you end up alone? How come the aliens didn't capture you?"

"I've been wondering that myself." Gears asked through the open channel.

Ben sat back, opening another juice container, but didn't immediately take a drink. "I ran and hid. I ran without direction, I just ran." His eyes were unfocused, his face a blank mask, no expression at all. "They had killed or captured the rest of the crew, I didn't know if they knew I was hiding or if they knew I was missing. I moved away from the wreck and followed a stream, I ran in the water, to use the sides of the stream as cover. There are a lot of streams and rivers around. A lot of water. I thought that was great, you know? Water means life, I figured there'd be fish, or lichens, or plants, or something." He shook his head sadly.

After a brief pause, he continued. "I found out there is no life on the planet's surface, at all. According to my instrumentations, the portable sensor I was able to take with me when I escaped, the water was safe to drink because it was sterile. Nothing grew on it, some minerals were in suspension or solution, but nothing toxic. I thought it was good news, at first, but then, I quickly found out there was no animal or plant life on the planet at all."

Ben took a long pull of the juice pack and was quiet for a while. First though he was done with his tale and was about to ask him a question when Ben started again.

"I made do with emergency rations and when I realized no rescue was coming in time for me not to starve or freeze to death, I decided to scout where the aliens were, where they had come from." He shook his head. "Boy was that a stupid thing to do. I found some caves, themselves the head of another river. Lots of solid rock all around, the entrance was relatively big, but the cavern inside was huge. Still, nothing alive in it. I found worked walls and an airlock at the end of a dog leg passage."

"You found what?" Noob's question echoed all around.

"There is a large airlock. Not a design I've ever seen. It must be their design, alien. It's huge." He paused and looked around. "You could probably put this shuttle through there and have room to spare."

"Where is it? Is it far?" First leaned forward and her sudden question made Ben jump.

"It's close to the hatch those missiles came from. About a kilometer further down." He shrugged, and then he sat forward, squinting his eyes. "What are you thinking?"

"We are going to take the fight to them, of course." Noob's grin went from ear to ear.

"The best defense is a good offense, you've heard that before, right?" Cap asked a pale and trembling Ben.

"You don't know what you are saying. There are a lot of aliens down below, I don't know how many, but a lot. It'd be suicide."

"No, not necessarily. We can plant explosives on the access points and close them down, that'll give us time to complete repairs and take off. Tactically, it's a sound plan."

"You are deluded. You are insane. You'll get us all killed." Ben raised his voice with each sentence and stood up on the last one.

"Sit down, Ben." Noob's hand clamped down on Ben's upper arm. "We are just talking here. We'll talk it out first."

Ben sat back down. "You didn't listen to me before, now we are in trouble. If you don't listen to me now, we'll be dead. Dead."

A loud alarm went off. Their sensors indicated movement all around Alfa.

"What the hell? Where did they come from?" Noob asked no one in particular.

"I'm reading multiple life signs approaching Alfa." Gears' voice, firm but worried came through the speakers. "They seem to have come out of the sand. I didn't get any readings. None. At all."

"Stealthy S.O.B.s" The calm in Cap's voice reigned in everyone's nervousness. "Welcome to the party, boys," Cap muttered under his breath.

"We have to go, whatever we can do, we must ..." Ben's face was bone-white, his eyes, wild. "What's the matter with you people? We are under attack, don't you understand?"

"Yes, we do. You don't." Cap calmly replied.

That's when the first explosion went off.

"They penetrated the minefield." Noob was up and moving with purpose towards the cockpit.

"Minefield? What minefield?" Ben was completely bewildered.

"You didn't think we'd just leave us vulnerable, after you telling us we had to be careful all this time, did you?" First asked him, with a smile as she, too, rushed off to the bridge.

Ben found himself alone in the galley, all others having darted off to the bridge. He felt as if he suddenly got shocked by a bolt of electricity and quickly got out of the bench and dashed to the bridge to join the crew there.

Ben ran onto the bridge to find Noob, Cap, and First at their stations, quietly talking to each other, taking readings, and paying attention to their instrumentation.

"Well, they got burned that time." Noob's smile was contagious.

"What did you do? How?" Ben was still in shock.

"Come on up. Take a look." Cap motions him to come over to the pilot area.

Ben could see outside of Alfa. There were many pieces, no other word for it, of aliens all around the ship. The sugar-white sand, heavily stained with blood, a deep dark purple, clearly not human, but disturbingly similar.

"They didn't breach the ship. Some made it all the way up to the hatches. The infantry point defense system took care of them. No breaches. No one made it inside." First matter of fact recitation impressed Ben. They were calm and cool. They must be worried, and even scared, but you could not tell by their demeanor or their actions, it gave him a little confidence that maybe, just maybe, he'd make it out of this after all.

Cap sat back on his chair. "Time to go on the offensive. We need to take them out or at least immobilize them so we can effect repairs and blast out of here." He looked around the bridge.

"Noob, Ben, and I will attack the alien's base. First you stay on the ship and complete whatever repairs you can. Also, keep an eye out for us. Gears, Second, you guys give us intelligence from your vantage point, too."

"Copy that." Gears rough voice came through the speakers.

"Well, Ben, it's payback time. You up to it?" Cap smiled.

"You bet I am." He nodded, lips pursed, quick and choppy up and down bobs of his head.

They got ready to hit the aliens, as hard as they could. That was the plan, anyway.

Chapter 5

First rerouted the sensors to her communicator. The hatch where the missiles originated closed back down tight, blocking any signal from alien town. Any movement would be relayed immediately to her by the sensors. She stopped by the armory and put on a tactical vest, strapped a blaster on her hip, another in a shoulder holster, and made sure she carried enough fully charged spare power packs for both.

She took a satchel and filled it with different odds and ends. She met the rest of the crew by the exit hatch and went out with Cap, Noob, and Ben, but split from them and headed for the still partially obstructed exhaust vents.

"You boys go and play. Bring me back something nice." She smiled and waved, making her way to the rear of the craft.

"Don't worry, we'll stop by the gift shop on our way out. We'll be back before you have a chance to miss us." Cap smiled back at her, waved, and they started the short drive to where they planned to deploy on foot, near the entrance Ben told them he discovered. They decided an approach on foot would be stealthier than going any closer in the all-terrain vehicle.

First chest expanded under the vest with a deep breath and let it out slowly, the cold air invigorating her. The stuff attached to the ship reeked as she approached. She tightened the respirator and the stench was filtered out. Hammering at the hard polymer was hard work, in a short time, sweat rolled off her, even though the temperature was quite low. Enough of it was off, so she walked the perimeter, supplementing the antipersonnel mines, making sure the perimeter was whole again.

She looked over her shoulder often. This was a weird world. The only sounds were the wind, and the sand when it fell and slid over itself. The eerie quiet made her jump at shadows. The frigid temperatures gave her goosebumps, too. Then again, the aliens came out of the ground and they never saw them coming. The sensors didn't either. She felt very much alone.

The grisly chore of picking up the alien remains and piling them between the Alfa and the wreck took a little time. Ben was right, although stained with purple blood, she could clearly tell the aliens were covered with fine white fur. Not very big, at least the pieces big enough for her to move, definitely smaller than a human. She couldn't tell anything about the way their faces looked, she didn't find one that was ... whole. Now, the remains were out of the field of fire of the shuttle's main weapons. All done, she walked around, surveying the ship before going back inside.

Taking the rest of that crap off will have to wait until we are back in the Einstein's Shadow.

A quick check of the sensors showed nothing, all quiet. She made multiple passes, the way the aliens had come up with no warning the last time, still fresh in her mind. "Sneaky bastards." She said out loud, although there was no one around to hear her.

She headed to the engine compartment. A smile peeked out of the corners of her lips. It'd been years since she worked engineering full time. All spacers have to go through all stations if they want to crew an interstellar ship, which made sense. Once in the pipe, the only people they could rely on were themselves. That was why regulations required any ship coming across a distress signal to stop and render aid unless there were attenuating circumstances. Also, it saved them from going mad with boredom, which was a plus. Any trip took years, all spacers spent a lot of time either learning a new facet of their life in space or honing their abilities.

She knew some people fell in love with one role or the other. Gears was an engineer through and through, he had no interest in command. He was passionate and dedicated to his engines. He was passionate and dedicated to the *Einstein's Shadow*, specifically. He had been with Cap for a long time.

She had done her stint in engineering on her previous ship. The same model engines, but fewer, adequate for a slightly smaller ship. She had come on the *Einstein's Shadow* as a Noob, but engineering rated. It hadn't bothered her, she wanted to command, which paid better.

The calculation for her was easy, her villa would be affordable in another seven or eight years, two or three more for pocket money. She had gone through all the command training, doing time as Noob, Second, and now, finally, as First. Larger ships had larger crews, but she enjoyed the smaller ships like the *Einstein's Shadow* better.

Checking the engines to determine if there was any additional damage due to the sudden increase in temperature and the failure to vent the exhaust, took a while but all readings came back OK. They would work, but ideally, she should clean the engines. Otherwise, because of the deposits on the ejection system, they would lose efficiency and would eventually overheat, compounding the problem. She dropped her toolbox, rolled up her sleeves, and got to work, mentally dusting off the many lessons learned on her previous ship. It wasn't hard work, as such, just tedious and physically demanding.

By the time she was done, morning was breaking and the white sand was shining brightly around most of the ship. The lack of insect or scavenger activity on the alien remains was unnerving, confirming what Ben said, there was no animal life at least on this side of the planet. The areas with the dried alien blood were a stark contrast to the white sand, a deep dark maroon, almost black. There were many such areas. Interestingly, it did not seep very deep, the sand must be finer than she thought. She gave her head a quick shake and started making sure they were ready to depart at a moment's notice.

CAP, NOOB, AND BEN approached the cavern Ben discovered slowly and carefully, but they couldn't find cover anywhere. They used the terrain as much as possible, but the dunes were not tall enough to help much. The river bed was a little more help, a little, not much.

As they approached, Cap used some of his equipment, which Ben identified correctly as military-grade battle sensors.

"Which outfit were you with?" Ben whispered. They were close to the cave and he didn't want to give their position away.

Cap shrugged, "I saw combat, I fought, the war ended. When we were disbanded, we were given some of our back pay in equipment. I have kept mine up to date, upgrading equipment as the opportunity arises or presents itself."

"Yeah, I don't think so. That is top-of-the-line, up-to-date equipment, and the blasters you people are wearing are new, all-terrain, all-weather blasters, multi-selector. I've only seen those in the news. There is nowhere a civilian can get his hands on one."

"Yes, there is." Cap smiled.

"Where? I don't believe you." Ben squinted his eyes.

"I have one, don't I? So obviously a civilian can have it."

"I still don't think that's right."

Noob put a heavy hand on Ben's shoulder. "Hey, Ben? Shut up. If Cap says it's cool, it's cool. You don't get to have an opinion."

That dried up the conversation, Ben followed them towards the opening, uneasily looking all around them.

They reached the alien's cave entrance, approaching it at an angle. Cap scanned and determined sensors effectively covered the mouth of the cave.

"They probably knew of your previous visit, I'm afraid. I wonder why they didn't go after you then?" He quietly told Ben as he manipulated his device.

"What are you doing now?" Asked Ben in a whisper, looking over Cap's shoulder at what he was doing.

"I'm remotely deactivating their sensor grid, giving a false *all OK* signal, the equipment is close enough to ours that I can hack it easily. Most are motion sensors or deal with infrared. We can talk, there are no microphone pick-ups." He smiled at Ben.

Ben's expression prompted Cap. "Most follow heat signatures. Makes sense, in this cool planet."

A frown blossomed on Ben's forehead; he was not buying it. Hacking equipment like that required highly sophisticated gear, not something you would expect on a cargo hauler, no matter how many of the crew were veterans.

"OK, I got them all. Let's go." Cap led the way into the cave.

The entrance was indeed relatively small, but it grew steadily in every direction soon after entering, the floor mostly leveled.

"Yeah, it looks natural, but it's fused rock. Aged artificially. The opening went all the way up at some point in the past. They closed the entrance top, making a sort of smaller access cavern." Cap described his readings in hushed tones as they carefully walked in. Gloom engulfed them the deeper in they went.

Noob, his head always in motion, his blaster ready, commented while examining their surroundings, "you know? They made a funnel, this is like a funnel, with a narrow end at the entrance. Do you think they want a choke point? That'd be weird."

Up ahead, the cavern turned slightly to the right.

"The dog leg you mentioned, I assume?" Cap turned back to Ben.

"Yes, the big hatch is about one hundred and fifty, maybe two hundred meters further in."

They kept going, slowly, quietly, taking advantage of any outcropping for cover. Once they turned the corner the light from the outside was all but gone. Their skin got covered in goosebumps from the sudden drop in temperature. The humid air was a sharp contrast to the cold dry air outside. Cap's equipment hadn't detected any more sensors. They slowly moved on.

Here the walls, floor, and ceiling were worked stone. Mostly smooth to the touch. Eventually, at the end of a fifty or seventy-meter arrow-straight passage, they came to the airlock.

Cap approached it cautiously and studied the imposing hatch door.

"Definitely of unknown origin. Their tech is just about on par with ours, by what I can determine. They have been here a while. A long while. I wonder why they haven't left?"

They searched further into an offshoot on the left, in oppressive darkness barely kept at bay by their flashlights. The cave, however, came to a dead-end rough-hewn wall twenty or thirty meters in.

They back-tracked to the antechamber where the big hatch was.

"We could go in; I could bypass the locking mechanism." Cap was examining the dull metal of the door and the surrounding edges merged with the stone wall. "I'm afraid, though, that we would alert the aliens in doing so, we don't have enough information. We might find ourselves helplessly outnumbered in an unknown area." He looked back at Noob and Ben.

They nodded at him. Noob and Cap paused to place a few charges around the hatch, and they started going back towards the entrance quietly.

"Terrific. I told you it was a bad idea to come here, we learned nothing." Ben was huffing and puffing as they hustled back to the entrance of the cave.

"Oh, we learned something, all right." Ben could see Cap's smile dimly in the light of their flashlights and the little outside light that now reached them.

"Really, Cap. Well, pray tell, what did we learn?"

"That the aliens are hiding there, they are sheltering. They have the tech to hide, we could not detect them until they opened their hatch, we couldn't penetrate this shielding either, they use it offensively. They seem to have made an airtight environment inside there. There are plenty of signs in an alien language all around." Ben turned his head every which way, not seeing anything. "Infra-red ink or paint. They are big on tracking or detecting heat. Might be something to keep in mind."

"Maybe they don't breathe this kind of atmosphere." Ben panted as he kept up with Cap and Noob as they finally made it out of the cave.

"The ones that came after us in the ship were not wearing environmental suits, they were breathing the atmosphere, if they breathe at all. They had exposed body surfaces. No, I don't think It's an atmosphere kind of thing. It's something else."

"Aliens are mysterious enough without loading further mysteries on them." Ben huffed.

"I would like an explanation." Cap shook his head, his brow furrowed, serious. They paused to place some more shaped charges around the cave mouth.

On their way back, they deviated and placed charges around the rock's top hatch.

They retreated to the all-terrain vehicle and headed for the ship.

The explanation for the hatch came, but not in a good way.

Chapter 6

First concentrated on rubbing the degreaser all over her hands. She was in the process of getting the mess off with a semi-clean towel when the sensor feed came through her communicator. Dropping the soiled rag in a nearby bucket with all the other ones she'd used in her repairs, she ran to the bridge.

A deep sigh escapes her when the life signs are human. Cap, Noob, and Ben are close enough for the sensors to detect, still no less than fifteen minutes away at the rate they are moving.

"Good to see you guys." She called out over the comm.

"Good to see Alfa." Cap panted into his communicator.

"Did you bring me anything?" She smiled at her own joke.

"No, the gift shop was closed and the only flowers available were wilted, sorry." A quick chuckle from Cap and the groan from Noob were both very welcome to First. Very happy they were back, the tension started to ease on her shoulders and back.

"Just come on over here, we are good to go as soon as you board." She made sure the outer hatch was ready to open, so they could come in quickly. She started the preflight sequence.

As the trio approached Alpha, she hit the hatch control and it opened, just in time for them to board.

"She warmed up?" Cap asked through the comm as he made his way to the bridge.

"And chomping at the bit. We can lift anytime." First answered on ship-wide.

Cap, Noob, and Ben spill into the bridge, immediately going to their stations to strap in.

Gears' rough voice burst loudly over the comm. "Brace, brace, brace."

Cap and First looked at each other, although Cap was already hitting the transmit button. "What the hell are you talking about? We are static on the ground, we read clear sky, no incoming."

"There is an energy wave on its way." Gears rushed words chase each other. "The system's star emitted the spike and will reach you in a few minutes. High intensity. Not going to be good. We may lose communications for a while." The litany of going through preflight on the *Einstein's Shadow* whispered in the background.

"I show nothing here." Frist was trying to locate the wave in her sensors with no success.

"It's all over the place, the radiation is ... not normal, not on the regular spectra." Second's words were clipped, urgent. "I don't know what the phenomenon is, I've never seen anything like it. The instruments on the stellar mapping probes say there is a massive energy wave coming, but we have nothing on any of the spectrophotometers, or any of the other sensors. The computer analysis speculates the ripple to be composed of a subatomic-particle wave moving at or very close to the speed of light. Possibly muon-neutrinos or tau-neutrinos. We think. Because we can't detect anything else, no charge, no mass registers in the sensors, just ... energy. This is beyond weird."

"How are you detecting anything if—" Ben asked from his supernumerary seat at the back.

"Never mind that. Are we properly shielded? Do we have time to move to a cave? Will the cave be shielding enough?" Cap asked, getting the ship ready to go.

"You should be ok. We think. We simply don't know." Second's swallowing was audible on the comm. "We believe the ship can take it. We just don't know."

"What are you going to do?" Cap asked in a leveled voice. Unperturbed. He was going through all the preflight and checking all the readings he could but in a fast, efficient manner.

"We'll be going into the shadow of one of the moons nearby, it's just about big enough to cover us." Second's voice was firm but rushed.

"OK. We'll be in touch when it's all over." Cap turned back to First and then to Noob. "First, activate the shields. I'm not sure lifting off is advisable. If this thing hits us and the shields can't take it, we might be worse off than riding it out on the ground." Cap wind down the preflight sequence.

"Shields active, Cap." First called from her station. Shields were the standard defense against energy weapons, such as lasers, phasers, and blasters. They weren't quite as effective against mass weapons, rail gun munitions, or missiles, for those, they had to use ECM or the point defense system. A trickle of sweat ran down her back, making her shiver.

A few minutes later the light show from the interaction of the shields with the subatomic particle wave was spectacular and terrifying. Normally the shields simply shimmer a little and their interaction with energy weapons results in a localized flash of white light. This time they were witness to an intense display of light. The shield showed its ovoid shape all around the ship, going into the ground around them. The experience was similar to being inside a pearl, looking at the shiny inside of the iridescent white surface. They stared at the phenomenon in fascination for some time.

As suddenly as it started, it ended.

Noob's shoulders relaxed as he let a deep breath out. "God, I didn't know if the shield was going to hold."

"I think it was a near thing." First was looking at the panel in front of her. "The batteries aren't depleted, but that's because they were full at the beginning of this. We would have had to run the engines on high if the wave kept it up for a few more minutes." She slumped back in her seat and rubbed her forehead, her heart slowing down somewhat. "That was close."

Cap was intently looking outside.

First turned to the pilot station, a frown wrinkled her forehead. "Cap? What's the matter?"

"Look over there." He pointed outside, towards some rock outcroppings.

The naked rock was now covered in fine dust, or sand, which the wind turned into a cloud that covered everything and made the sky a light pinkish color.

"You think the rock is red?" Noob asked as he admired the brief reddish clouds the wind created.

"No, I think it's a refraction thing." Cap was now looking at the immediate area around the ship, his face lost all color.

"Cap? What's the matter? What do you see?" First looked out too, Noob and Ben walked up to look outside.

The area outside the shields where the alien's blood had spilled now had nothing on it but fine sugar-white sand, which they all now conclude must be ash. Some of the blood still stained the ground where the shields protected it, but now a dark brownish color rather than the previous maroon apparently cooked through. The alien remains between Alfa and the wreck outside the shield were simply gone, reduced to ... ash. It became evident to them, even if no one mentioned the fact, the radiation destroyed biological tissue.

First sat at her station. "*Einstein's Shadow*, this is Alfa, come in." She tried for a few minutes but no response from the ship came through.

"Let's blast off this planet. Come on guys, you have to agree now that staying here is beyond dangerous." Ben's pleading voice broke into the stillness of Cap and Noob's concentrated labors and First monotonous calls.

Cap turned to First. "I need a sensor reading of the last location of the *Einstein's Shadow*. Where is it?"

First frantically studied her sensor displays, her forehead creased, her fingers dancing all over her station. "I can't get any readings. The wave of ... stellar material, I guess, is a sphere moving away from the star. I can read everything inside it, but nothing out of it. The *Einstein's Shadow* is beyond the sphere. It's dispersing, I think, but very slowly." Her hands turned up and out, as she shook them in frustration before going back to the sensor suite. "I can't even read the outer planets. I can't ... wait. I'm getting something now. Yes, I can read one of the planets and I'm getting some more data from the outer orbits. The sphere is dissipating."

"Thank God." Noob's heartfelt comment reflected what they all were thinking.

"Got it. I got the *Einstein's Shadow* signal. Still behind the moon, but they are making their way over to the other side, I guess he's going to have to orbit around it to turn around if he is going to his previous stellar synchronous orbit."

"...can you hear me. Please, come in. Shuttle Alfa, this is—"

"Second, I copy, I copy." First tense body relaxed hearing the voice of her shipmate. "We are OK."

A clapping sound proper of an enthusiastic high five came clearly over the static of the open channel.

"Thought we had lost you for a minute there." The unmistakable gravel voice of Gears broke through the static.

"Same here. We couldn't make you out for a while either." Cap's relief was evident in his voice.

"Yes, well, the damn thing is dissipating. Can barely read it already and it's not even beyond the outer planet's orbit. I can detect it now only because I know what I'm looking for."

"I can't detect it either." First frown was back as she tried unsuccessfully to recuperate the signal trail of the energy wave.

"We are on our way back to the previous orbit unless you want us somewhere else Cap?"

"No, go back." Cap put his knuckles to his mouth and bumped it a couple of times, pensive. "First, get me a status on Alfa. Run a full diagnostic. Noob, make sure the buoy is transmitting, see if it suffered any damage from the energy wave. We are not taking any chances; we get Alfa ready and we bug out."

"About time." Exclaimed Ben as he slumped on his seat.

They all got to work and got ready to leave immediately. Of course, the aliens had other ideas.

Chapter 7

The systems check came back normal, there was no detectable damage to the ship or its instrumentation.

"Why are we bothering with the buoy?" Ben exasperatedly raised his voice. "I told you, we marked the wreck when we got here, the aliens came out and simply took it. I guess to use the tech and to continue luring others down here."

"Maybe so, but we are making sure our buoy is operational, and then we will leave. It's already in place, we just have to make sure it's transmitting. We will claim the salvage rights in Mobula 3, but also the signal will prevent others from coming to the rescue signal. A win-win." Cap shrugged his shoulders.

"I don't know." Ben scratched his chin. "We were on our way to Mobula 3 also, but we diverted here when we picked up the distress signal and, well, clearly we never made it out. Our buoy got taken by the aliens, and you were lured here."

"How long have you been here?" Noob asked without lifting his head from his console.

"By the planets count, five weeks. As far as I'm concerned, forever."

"Noob, what do you read over there?" First asked never taking her eyes from her instrumentation.

"No damage, nothing major anyway. We should change some of the shield emitters, just in case, I mean, we cooked them with that prolonged ship-wide energy barrage."

"Cap? What do you want us to do? Do we swap them out now or do we wait until we are out of here?"

"I don't want to be out in space, have the aliens show up with energy weapons, and find that the shield has a weak area or a hole in it because of something we could have done here. Swap them out, but let's be quick about it." Cap didn't look up, he kept working his station.

"Noob, you are with me." First headed out.

"First, let's split up, you do the inside and I'll do the outside." Noob picked up the replacement emitters from storage.

"No, very gallant of you, but no. If I'm outside with you, we'll finish in less than half the time."

"Hey."

"I'm not saying I work faster than you, which I do." Her smile teased him even more. "But we won't need to be going from one side of Alfa to the other. You take port, I'll take starboard, we both start at the prow and we'll be done in no time."

"Yeah, it makes sense. OK."

They affected the repairs on the hull and then checked for any additional damage on the outside. Nothing else amiss, they rushed back in.

Noob called in on the comm before going in. "Cap, I'm checking the perimeter. Do you want me to pull it back, disarm all the mines and bring them in?"

Cap sat back from his station. Shook his head and pressed the transmit button. "No, Noob, leave them. If we think we'll have time, we'll pick them up, but otherwise, let's leave them. I would not want to have an attack right when we are lifting off and have the mines in the war chest, being useless."

"Copy that. On my way in."

First brought the ship analyzer online, her eyes fixed on the read-out.

"First, what's the holdup back there?" Cap's voice through the ship-wide was urgent, loud, and clear.

"I brought back a little of the sand and the dust covering the ship. I'm running it through the analyzer while Noob boards. The sand is mostly finely crushed rock. It would seem the portion of the high-energy wave that gets through the atmosphere literally pulverizes the exposed rock surfaces. That's why the planet gives the impression of an interminable desert." She answered closing the analyzer and rushing to the bridge.

"Certainly, seems to be the explanation of why we found no life on the planet." Cap turned as First entered.

"Let me check the river's origin, the one we detected in the orbital passes. If there is life anywhere, it would probably be at the river head, protected by rock, but with available water and solar radiation."

She manipulated the sensors, although detecting anything inside a cave from this far away would be difficult.

"Nothing. There is no detectable life, at least, not from here." She was curious and would like to check it out in closer inspection, but the risk was not worth the effort.

"Who cares about that?" Ben's raised voice resonated through the bridge.

"We need to know as much as we can before we go." Cap calm response had a steadying effect on Ben. "We need to know as much as we can so we can detail what happened on the planet and what to expect when they come here on our report in Mobula 3." He never looked up from the final stages of getting Alfa ready for departure.

"So? What's the big deal? What if there's life? Or if there isn't life? What's the relevance?"

Cap turned slowly towards Ben, done with his console, just waiting for Noob and First to finish their preflight. "Inhabitants of a planet need to live off the planet. If there is nothing but those aliens alive on this planet, they are probably visitors, not indigenous. It also means that they are either waiting to be rescued or have given up on being rescued. That, in turn, means that their sealed habitat must be self-sufficient. Either way, it gives us insight into what we are up against."

Ben's eye roll made clear what he thought of Cap's argument. "Listen, can't we do all that from orbit? Or better yet, can't we leave this whole mess for the next people that come, preferably armed to the teeth?"

"No, I don't like turning and running without information. Otherwise, it might be a short run." Cap returned to his console.

"Ben, leave it alone. We'll be in the air in a couple more minutes. Take it easy." Noob tried to reason with him.

"I just want out of this damn planet," Ben murmured under his breath.

"We all do." Commented Noob, louder, winking at him.

Chapter 8

"Point defense system online?" Cap asked as Alfa trembled on takeoff.

"Ready, willing, and able." Noob replied enthusiastically. He wanted payback.

First eyes were glued to the sensors. They had decided to leave the security perimeter they set up in place. If the aliens came across it after they took off, well ... it'd be messy, for sure, at least until the next solar flare. She hoped she didn't find out at all. She wanted to put this place firmly in the 'memories not to be open' compartment of her mind. She sat up with a start.

"I have movement. An energy spike from the alien town hatch."

"Now we see if our parting gifts work as intended."

Noob nodded at Cap's comment but kept his eyes on the fire control readings, they were not going to be caught flat-footed again.

The rocky outcropping that served as the missile staging area for the aliens started to open. The thunderous explosions blew boulders and what the sensors indicated were refined and worked metal fragments high in the air. Nothing was going to be launching from there anytime soon.

"The opening is collapsing. Your explosive precaution was very effective." First was smiling again.

"We'll make it into orbit this time, right?" Ben's trembling voice and white-knuckled grip on his chair made it clear he was terrified again.

"Well, that will depend on—"

"We got movement on the far side of alien town from you. Seems to be ..." Gears voice on comms hesitated.

"I'm reading the spike. Damn, another hatch. We didn't detect this one, Cap." First shook her head in disbelief and frustration.

"Well, we know what's coming. Noob, get on station."

"On it, Cap. I'm ready, let'em come."

Three paired missile volleys made their way to them.

First sensors picked them up. "I got them. The first four, two sets of two, fifteen seconds apart, seem to be the same kind they hit us with last time. The other two are different, bigger, but I can't penetrate the casing, I'm unable to determine if they are explosive or incapacitating ordinance."

"Taking evasive action. I don't think the inertial dampers are going to be sufficient, get ready for some G's." Cap's warning was timely, they immediately felt the effects of the aggressive maneuvers.

Noob fixed the anti-missiles sights on the incoming. "Firing."

He scored one hit on the first pair, and both missiles exploded, a dense cloud of goop expanding on their trajectory.

He scored again, this time hitting both missiles of the second salvo.

The third pair had countermeasures of their own and intercepted his fire.

"Cap, you better get us out of here. I can't get a solid fix on these guys."

"I'm driving the bus, kid, I'm driving the bus." His teeth clenched.

Suppressing fire from a rotating point defense system gun finally took one of the missiles down. The explosion threw them into their harnesses.

"Keep them away from us for a minute longer, Noob, just one more minute." Cap's clipped words were barely loud enough for Noob to hear.

He evaded the missile once, twice, three times. Each time it overshot, it turned around and came back, relentless and mindlessly chasing them.

"It better run out of fuel soon." Murmured Cap.

"Why?" Cried Ben from the back. "What's wrong now?"

"Shut up, Ben." Noob bit out, intent on his defense systems.

"More incoming. These are different again." First hands flew over the controls, trying to identify the nature of the new threat.

"OK, there must be something amiss with the guidance system, they will miss us completely, they will overshoot one on each side."

"I don't like it." Grumbled Cap.

"You don't like being missed when shot at? I like it better when they miss, what are you talking about Cap?" Ben's strident voice was getting on everyone's nerves.

"Something is wrong. First, what can you tell me about the incoming, the new ones?" Cap kept his aggressive evasive actions, but the missiles matched his maneuvering turn by turn.

"Nothing. They are ... different. Unknown tech, I can't determine what kind of payload they have. They will miss us though, they are wide. They are fast alright, they will overtake us."

"I'm taking us down."

"Are you insane?" Ben's voice went up an octave.

"I'll maneuver over that ridge, come back over, and climb over the wreck."

"Copy, I'll keep the stubborn little guy entertained, he won't catch us." Noob concentrated on the obstinate missile that refused to break target lock.

"OK, this is officially creepy. The incoming are altering their course, still nowhere close, but will flank us in a few seconds."

"No they won't," Cap pushed the engines even more.

"Cap, you are redlining the engines. Remember we still have some of that stuff on the exhaust." First kept a wary eye on the engine's temperature.

"Can't be helped."

Assisted by gravity, their dive now had them outpacing all three incoming.

"I think we are in the clear." The elation in Noob's voice was refreshing.

"The big ones are leveling above our altitude, opening up, will be on top of us soon, but nowhere near us." First kept her eye on the engine temperature.

Alfa lost a little speed as it leveled off.

"Got it!" Noob exclaimed triumphally as he finally got the trailing missile.

"The other two are overshooting us, their altitude steady, they are ..."

Both missiles exploded. The debris cones projected towards each other, effectively covering Alfa in the fast advancing cloud.

"What the hell is that?" Cried Ben.

The turbulence shook Alfa like a dog would a rag doll. Only the harnesses stopped them all from spilling to the floor.

"I have it. I have it." Called out Cap as he wrestled the controls.

They lose altitude fast.

All went dark. Alfa lost all power.

A collective groan broke the sudden silence engulfing them.

"Brace for impact." Called out Cap. His desperate maneuvers brought them once more over the dune near the wreck. Lights flickered back on as power came back online and Cap pulled up at the last minute, but the engines were not answering consistently. "I have to put her down, fast."

Rough maneuvers that threw them against their harnesses mercilessly brought them to a controlled crash landing not far from their previous position.

"Well, that was exciting. What's next on the program?"

"Don't be flippant, Noob. That one was too close for comfort. We are in real trouble."

"I know Cap, but I'd rather laugh than cry." He pointed with his thumb towards Ben, who seemed to be quietly sobbing into his hands.

"I'm running diagnostics. There seems to be no major damage to the ship. Like last time, we are incapacitated, but the ship is still functional."

"What's wrong with us this time?" Cap unstrapped himself and moved to First station.

"All I can tell you is that whatever they covered us with shorted our power. It was more like it grounded everything and tripped all the safeties. They came back up, of course, but effectively they had us without power for a few seconds, so we fell like a stone."

"How? How did they do that? Can you tell from the readings?" Cap rubbed his forehead.

"I have no idea. I mean, I guess there are ways we could rig something like that up, but it would take time. I guess they know enough about our ships to make offensive weapons that incapacitate without destroying us. Or scavenged the tech from some other victims, we can't know at this point."

Cap scratched his head. "Yes, but why? Why not just hit the engines and take us down?"

"They took my crewmates. They may not only want the technology; they may also want the crew." Ben commented between desperate sobs.

"Creepy, but possible. OK, what do you think, First?" Cap shook his head and pursed his mouth.

"I need a little time."

"Alfa, come in. What is going on? Are you all alright? We saw you blow the enemy spider hole and saw them shoot at you. You are down, but you read OK."

Cap clicked the comm. "We are OK, Gears, but grounded at the moment. Any further movement you can detect?"

"No, they opened the port just long enough for the missiles to launch. Then they closed it tight. We have a fix on it, but no further reading. It's like it's not even there."

"Cap, I think we can fix Alfa no problem, a couple of areas overloaded, but nothing we can't fix. We have the parts; all we need is time."

"All we need is time? Have you not been paying attention? The aliens will come back and keep coming until they capture us all." Ben's eyes were red-rimmed and his nose inflamed, but at least he was not crying anymore.

"Cap?" Gears' voice was hesitant over the comm. "We could take Beta down. Second can man the defense system, I can have Alfa up and running in no time. Then, we can lift off together. Alfa is a harder target, but Beta is a lot quicker. We can hit them hard and they'll never be able to touch us."

Cap sat back on his chair. All eyes were on him, but all waited patiently for him to decide.

"Tough call. If the aliens pull new tricks out of their hat, we might lose both shuttles and be stranded here, with *Einstein's Shadow* up in orbit on autopilot. There's the cargo earmarked for Mobula 3 to think off too. No. We'll deal with it ourselves."

"I'm going out and repositioning the perimeter. I want an alarm system in case our hosts decide to drop by." Noob stood up and exited the bridge.

"I'll start the repairs in here. It's all minor, but there's a lot of it."

"First, I'd rather you take the engines, I'll deal with the circuitry here. We'll meet midship."

"Let's go." First pulled Ben up.

"Me?"

"Yeah, you can help me and I'd like more of your story."

"Whatever you want, just ask." Ben's voice was low, passive.

"I want to know why the aliens seem to want the hardware, but what is really making me uneasy is that I think you are right. I think they want us, too, not just our tech."

"They do." Ben kept walking back.

Ben seemed to know more than what he'd told them. First shook her head, a lot was going on here, and they were missing pieces. Important pieces, missing from the puzzle.

Chapter 9

"Pass me that wrench, the adjustable one." First pointed to a tool partially under one of the engine covers on the floor. "Time to come clean, Ben. Tell me about your time on the planet. The whole thing, don't leave anything out."

Ben let out a deep breath. "Like I told you guys before. We were on our way to Mobula 3 for business. We were going to lease out some designs for 3D printing, also we had some franchise opportunities for any interested parties. You know, the standard trip to a frontier world." He shrugged.

First nodded and continued to work the engine. "Tell me about your getting here. What happened? Exactly."

Ben sat back on his haunches. "We came down, much as you guys did, but with our ship. Ours was a smaller passenger ship, our crew was just five people, and we were ten passengers. The crew," he smiled at the memory, "everyone was very excited when they received the signal. They were all thinking about the money they'd make. I ... we were on this trip to make money too, so we figured, you know, if it was a big enough find, then all fifteen of us could make some serious money. The crew was all for sharing, they'd split whatever we got half for the crew, and half would be for us, the passengers. So we agreed." He absentmindedly picked up a screwdriver and started twirling it. "It sounded like easy money, you know? It sounded simple. Safe."

First finished the repair and put the cowling back on. "Let's move over here." She pointed with the wrench. "Then what happened? Details, I want details."

Ben shook his head and dropped the screwdriver into the toolbox. "We landed. Close to here, right up next to the wreck. We already knew it was several different ships, but didn't figure out why. We couldn't, really, at that time. When we started investigating ... we found ... I found a strong room. It was filled with jewelry. It had a solid, strong door. It must have been a secure room on the ship before the crash. The door was intact, the locking mechanism was intricate, and it was open, unlocked, just ajar. I called them all. We had found ... a lot of money. A lot." He smiled. "Not on Mobula 3, of course, they don't have the means to waste on jewelry, they are eking out a living, barely. However, when we returned, in the rim worlds, what was in the vault would be worth a fortune many times over. All of us would be rich."

First pulled the other coaling off and was working on the starboard engine. "Was that when you got attacked?"

"No. We placed the buoy, a location buoy, coded for our ship. We deactivated the distress signal and retreated to the ship. We figured we would stop on the way back and pick it all up. We took some, not a lot, but some, of the basic pieces we figured we could perhaps sell or barter in Mobula 3. The rest we were counting on picking up on our way back. We had thought of getting an external cargo pod in Mobula 3 and on our way back ..." Ben grew quiet for a bit, lost in thought, and shrugged.

First finished with the engine and moved to the console to run tests. "When were you attacked?"

"We got on the ship, closed her up, and took off, we were ready to celebrate as soon as we got on the pipe. We were all happy, you know?" He shook his head, and his hands rubbed his face forcefully. "That's when it happened. They shot us down the same as you. Except we weren't as quick to land. The engines were damaged, from overheating. We could repair them, of course, but it would take time. Time they didn't give us." He stood up and walked away from her, leaning his back on the wall, hands in his pockets. "They came out of the sand, just like they did this time, we never saw them coming. We tried to repel them, but all we had on board was a few projectile weapons. We scattered, they breached the hatch, they blew it open. I ... I was so scared. I hid in the cargo hold. I picked up whatever survival gear I could find and some rations and I sneaked out through a side cargo hatch."

First ran tests and listened attentively to the story. "What can you tell me about the aliens?"

Ben stood up straight. "Smaller than us, a little, like maybe a head smaller, on average. Solid, though, just as wide. Muscular, too. They all had dull silver clothing, I guess that's a way to blend with the sand out there." He pointed with his thumb in the general direction of the outer hatch. "They have light gray fur everywhere their skin showed. Two cat-like eyes, you know, with slit pupils. Their ears, on top of their heads, have little tufts of hair. The silver clothing must be bullet-proof. We shot them, but none of them went down. None. They kept coming." He shook his head again.

"You got a very good look at them." First commented from where she was running tests.

"Well, yeah, I mean, I saw them, and is not like they were hiding or anything." A short, sharp head shake. "They rounded us all up, and they took everyone with them. I hid in the rock outcropping ..." Ben paused to get his bearings and pointed to one of the walls. "Over there. I had a clear line of sight on the ship. They came in several ground vehicles, of different sizes, and designs. Weird, you know? Like they were from different planets. They took the crew. I tried to follow, but couldn't, they were too fast for me, so I came back. I picked up a few more things I figured I'd need to survive on the planet. Then went out and hid nearby."

"They didn't leave a guard back on your ship?"

"No, they thought they had all of us, so, no need, I guess. Anyway, later, they came back, looted, and disassembled the ship. Took a lot of the parts on cargo vehicles, and the rest they simply incorporated into the wreck. They reactivated the emergency beacons and left." He sighed and shook his head again, falling silent.

First turned to him. "What did you do then?"

"I followed the tracks, as carefully as I could, keeping to the streams and riverbeds. It was easy, some of the cargo vehicles used caterpillar tracks, so they were easy to follow on the sand. I found the entrance to the cave. I couldn't approach it. I was too scared. I retreated and tried to survive. There is nothing to sustain life on this planet. Nothing. In the end, I went to their cave, to try to sneak in. The hatch is impenetrable. I came back out and hid in a deep cave I found before, it has a river coming out of it so I was relatively safe and, you know, I had water. I came out days later, desperate, ready to go back to the alien's cave to find out if there was a way to sneak in or something when I saw you guys."

"That's an interesting story, but nothing helps me." The harsh statement made Ben visibly wince.

"Sorry. That's all I know. I don't even know where they have my crewmates. They must be in their cave, but ..." his hands came up, palm up.

"First, how are we looking back there? I read the engines ready to go here." Cap's voice came loudly ship-wide.

"We are ready. Just let me tighten everything and we are a go."

"Copy that, come on up here, let's blow this place."

First fastened everything and rechecked that all tools were stowed away safely. "Let's go, Ben. Let's get off this rock."

"Music to my ears."

They rushed to the bridge.

Cap was already strapped in, as was Noob. "Get your buts on the chairs and strap in, we are taking off rough."

They had barely finished tightening their restraints when Alfa leaped in the air.

At that exact moment, the sensor grid went off.

"Sneaky bastards!" First said through clenched teeth. "A lot of them, this time we are talking a whole lot of them."

"I see them." Noob was already firing their outside cannons.

The defense perimeter erupted in explosions triggered by the advancing aliens.

"I bet that hurt them." Cap smiled, his voice soft and steady.

"Incoming." First hands frantically worked the console in front of her. "They are heat seekers, and they are locked on good." A frown creased her forehead.

"Let's find out if I can shake them." Cap went into desperate evasive maneuvers.

"I can't hit the ground troops consistently like this." Noob's voice calm and steady, although his hair was damp and sweat was rolling down his cheeks.

"Let them be. I think we are almost out of ..." Cap paused and performed an abrupt maneuver.

Two of the missiles missed them cleanly and went off, having lost lock on their engines.

"Good one, Cap, but we have two more on our tail." First looked up, Ben trembled strapped in his seat, hands on his lap, eyes wide open, mouth closed in a straight thin line. "Damn. Two more in the air. They are not playing around this time, they are trying to bring us down, I don't think these are incapacitating ordinance, I think they mean to blast us."

"Let's return the compliment." Cap performed a barrel roll and inverted.

Noob didn't need to be told to shoot. As soon as he had a clear field of fire, he strafed the ground troops effectively. "Take that!"

The explosion shook Alfa.

"Where did that come from?" for the first time Cap's words were angry and loud.

"I don't ... They shot at us as we were diving to attack, I never saw it." First bitterness dripped from every word.

"It was a rhetorical question. Don't sweat it." Cap was fighting to regain control of Alfa.

Noob continued targeting as many clusters as he could, but his fire was less than effective, given the abrupt maneuvers from Cap.

"I can't hold it. We are going down."

"Cap. First. We are getting Beta ready, we have her loaded for bear. They're gonna find out they can't mess with us." Gears' voice thundered from the speakers.

"No. Gears do not come to try a rescue, I repeat do not come down to the planet. The capabilities of the enemy are unknown and we can't risk you too. Stay up in stellar orbit, I don't think they have detected you. Now shut up and let me fly this thing."

A cold shiver went down First's spine. She had never heard Cap ask for time to pilot or take care of anything. Things must be really bad. She sneaked a quick look at the status board and the readings froze the blood in her veins. They were down to less than ten percent power. It was going to be a close thing, to land and not crash.

Cap finally stabilized their dive and pulled the nose up, banking away from the alien forces.

Noob jumped over to a second console.

"What are you doing?" Yelled First. "Strap down. At this speed the dampeners can't handle the load, you will be thrown around like playing dice in a cup."

"I just need to... There. Eat that!"

A missile dropped from Alfa and activated a few feet below them. Flying straight and true towards the enemy position.

"Three, two, one. Boom." Noob's last word coincided with the huge explosion that took out the vanguard of the enemy.

The rest of the ground force beat a hasty retreat.

"Well, that bought us some time." Cap was looking franticly at the different instruments.

"What do you need?" Asked First, sensing his intentions.

"Somewhere we can set up a hard position, where they can't reach us."

"Scanning."

"How can I help?" Gear's question broke in the momentary silence.

"Start prepping to leave the system and going on to Mobula 3." Cap's clipped response prompted Ben to regain his voice.

"What in God's name are you talking about? They can't leave!"

"Neither can we, apparently." Said Cap, concentrating on his readings and showing the strain of keeping Alfa in the air. "I need a place to land this bird. Now would be good."

"I think I have a place. A little longer flight, sending the data to your screen." First was frantically working her station.

"Got it. We can make it. Maybe."

"We are all going to die here." Ben's murmured statement was loud enough for all to hear, but no one chose to answer.

"I can't keep it in the air any longer. I have to land." Cap lined Alfa with a ridge a little further up. "Brace."

The landing was bumpy, but nothing broke or buckled.

"What about our friends? Any pursuit?" Noob asked, checking his weapons station.

"No. I don't detect anything, but then again, they seem to be able to sneak up close and personal before we read them. The scopes are clear though, I can read them where we left them. I think your last punch gave them a bloody nose." First turned and smiled at Noob.

"This is no laughing matter." Screamed Ben. "If we don't leave we'll die."

"And we can't leave, so we have to find an alternative." Cap addressed the comm. "Gears? Start prepping to get back on the pipe. Keep a sharp eye out for incoming. They have not targeted you guys yet, but I don't want any surprises."

"Cap, I wouldn't feel right leaving you–"

"Listen. These guys have this planet figured out. They have not blown us out of the sky. They haven't gone after you, so either they don't know about you, or can't reach you. Either way, the *Einstein's Shadow* can't help down here, and neither can Beta." He hastened to add. "They'd just blast it out of the sky and then we'd all be stranded. Our best bet is for you to go and bring help if it comes to that."

"I don't like it, but you are the Captain."

"Glad we agree, then," Cap smirked. "I know it's a bitter pill. Give us some time, we'll see if we can sort this out. We'll be in touch, keep an eye out for incoming both up there and around us."

"Copy that."

"That's three to four YEARS we will never survive that long." Ben was in hysterics.

"We can't leave, every time we try, they come after us with more force. We don't know their capabilities, but we do know they want to salvage, at least, some parts of the ship, we need more intelligence and we need a better defense. Besides, it'll be more like two years, tops." Cap nodded reassuringly.

"What about living on this God-forsaken planet. There is no food. Nothing. I found out first hand, I tried living here, it can't be done."

Cap shrugged. "The aliens live here. They may have found life under the surface. We need more intelligence."

First didn't see it, herself. They have food for a few weeks, maybe a few months, yes, if rationed, but the main problem would be the power for the blasters and other weapons. If they had to stay here and wait for the *Einstein's Shadow* to reach its destination and send help, they would be stranded here for years. It didn't look viable to her, but she trusted Cap. He had never let her down before.

Chapter 10

Noob, First, and Ben made quick work of fixing Alfa up.

"She's not orbital capable right now." Noob got the last of the grime from his hands with a rag.

"We don't need her to be. Not at this time. We just need her to be maneuverable enough to reach the rock formation I detected. It seems to have a blind cave, large enough for Alfa, and the river coming out means we'd have water, so I think it'd be an adequate place to take cover while we make her spaceworthy again."

"You guys are deluded. If we don't blast off this God-cursed planet soon, they will capture us. They can, you know. They will. I thought you guys would save me, but all you have done is run around, take off and crash. We are doomed." Ben finished cleaning his hands, slid down the wall until he sat on the floor, and rested his forehead on his arms.

First turned to Noob, who shrugged.

"Cap? Try her, she should be OK now."

"Copy." The quiet rumble of the engines was a reassuring sound. "Come on up, First, let's hop over to that rock you found. Noob, take Ben to the hold, open the war chest, I want a perimeter as soon as we land. I don't want any more surprises."

"Sir."

Ben's head came up, he glanced around, shook his head, and got up, his silence spoke volumes. They all head out to accomplish their tasks.

They strapped in.

"Here we go." Cap brought Alfa up on a vertical take-off.

"Company." First called out as soon as they left the ground. "They are cresting the dune now, several vehicles, all seem armed. We'll have incoming in a few seconds."

"No, we won't." Noob's voice was firm and steady. The front cannons of Alfa barked twice and the incoming vehicles were destroyed in impressive explosions that quickly turned into balls of fire and black smoke. Those following the lead vehicles overturned, making the rest of them deviate. The alien advance stopped cold, while they dismounted and took care of their wounded.

"What on Earth did you hit them with?" Asked a surprised and relieved First.

"It wasn't me. They must have had explosives on the vehicles, I'm loaded with regular antipersonnel ammo."

"All right, I'll take any good news at this point. Here we go." Cap said again.

The quick hop was over in a few minutes. Thankfully, there was no sign of further pursuit.

"Keep an eye out, I'll back us in." Cap concentrated on the readings, the cave was massive but will leave little extra room after Alfa was inside it.

The front of Alfa was just a little outside of the cave, but it was protected on the sides, above, and behind by thick solid stone walls. The armament was perfectly usable, and the field of fire was optimal for defense. They were on a small rise of the terrain, so anyone approaching could be seen from far away.

"Home sweet home." Cap turned to Noob and First, "you guys go out and set up a defense perimeter. I want you both in full tactical gear, blasters, and carabines."

"You got it." Noob jumped out of his seat closely followed by First.

They loaded up with everything they needed quickly and efficiently. All those nonsense drills paying off and then some.

They quickly established a wide, multilayered defense perimeter around the mouth of the cave.

Next, they climbed the formation and placed sensor arrays and several of Cap's 'party favors' on the rock formation's top and sides. Anyone coming at them from behind would have a few nasty surprises for sure.

"We are secure." First told Cap as she walked on the bridge.

"I can read the sensors up top. Three sixty overlapping sensor grids. All up and running. OK, Ben, you are with me, let's take a walk around our new home." Cap got up and headed aft.

"Why would we want to explore the cave? I told you, nothing lives on this planet. It's an empty cave, what do you expect to find?"

Cap stopped and slowly turned to Ben. "We need to know that there are no soft spots on the walls that can be capitalized by the enemy, we need to see where the stream originates, having water near is quite useful. We need to make sure there are no entrances we did not detect. Oh, yes, I almost forgot. I'm the Captain, and I said so." He smiled as he said the last, but it was cold and humorless.

Ben scratched the back of his neck and looked around at the rest of the crew, all of whom were looking back at him, neither of them with any sympathy.

"OK, sorry." Muttered Ben and headed out, following Cap.

Noob let out a chuckle. "I thought Cap was going to smack him."

"Nah, he's too cool for that. He'll make him sorry for it, I'm sure, but nothing as crude as beating him up." First was sure Ben would soon realize Cap knew better than him. Than any of them.

"CAP? SORRY ABOUT THAT, I didn't mean any disrespect." Ben's voice echoed from the walls at the back of the cave. No light reached the back with Alfa blocking the entrance.

"It's OK. Don't do it again and we'll get along great." Cap answered absentmindedly, examining the walls both visually and with the handheld scanner. "These are solid. Sturdy and thick. I don't think we have anything to worry about in this area." He patted the walls hard. "Weird that there is no life here, no insects, nothing."

"Well, that's good in a sense, no risk of insect bites or whatever, right?"

"Yes. Have to look at things in the best light."

They reached the origin of the stream. A spout of water came out of the ground, close to the end of the cave.

"Well, the sensor indicates the water does not extend under the outer wall, rather the big pool is under us, as it were. So the bad guys can't gain entrance through the stream. The outer wall here is relatively thin." He studied the reading deep in thought. "Still, it should hold, or make enough noise to alert us. Let's get back."

"So that's why you wanted to explore the cave. You wanted to know if the stream originated in the cave, or if it originated outside and the aliens could make it in through it." Ben shook his head. "I didn't think of that." He murmured to himself.

Cap winked, smiled, and walked back to Alfa.

"You boys had a fun time exploring the cave?"

"Yes, First, it was a nice spelunking outing." Cap's smile illuminated his face as he entered the bridge. "How are we looking here?"

"All clear. The sensors are working, our friends haven't even tried to come close. I think they are not used to getting punched back."

Noob turned to Cap. "Actually, I think they are not used to people putting up a fight. I think they are used to surprising people and getting away with a blitz attack."

"Could be. Let's not take anything for granted. Let's go to the galley. I want to make an inventory and figure out how long we can last. First, send all sensor data to the galley, I want you with us too."

"Sir."

They headed back to figure out if waiting a couple of years for the *Einstein's Shadow* to come back was advisable, or even possible.

Chapter 11

"Gears, we'll give this a little more time. We'll prep Alfa. If we decide we can make it out, we'll go up. If we decide we can't run away from these guys, you go on to Mobula 3 and bring back help."

"I don't know, Cap. I'd rather come down with Beta and fly cover while you guys take off."

"And if they shoot you down too, then we are done because no one will be able to come back to rescue us. No. We'll try to escape, if we can't, you go on."

"You are the Captain."

"While we are all online, let's examine the recordings we made of the alien's cave"

The rock walls were clearly labeled under infrared light. The language was unknown, but there were large and small characters, and some graphics, it was evident to anyone who could see in those wavelengths.

"Do the aliens see in IR?" Noob asked aloud, to no one in particular.

"I moved in the river beds for cover, most of the time inside the streams and rivers themselves, and they are cold. Do you think that's why I could escape? Do you think we can evade them using the rivers?"

"It's something to keep in mind. Also, it might explain why the alien fire was concentrated in the engine exhaust, the hottest part of the ship." Noob pointed out.

"Nah, we have heat seekers too, and we see in several wavelengths, I don't think we can use that as an explanation. Let's concentrate on what we know and not speculate." First smiled to make sure they knew she wasn't disparaging, "although I agree that it is something we should examine."

"OK, now let's–"

A blaring warning signal sounded all over Alfa.

First called up the information on the galley's monitor. "Incoming. They are coming at us hard, three vehicles that I can make out. Straight for the back door. They obviously don't want to engage directly."

"Let's crew the defenses and–"

"Cap, wait. They stopped. Well out of range."

"That's weird." Noob's puzzled comment reflected what they all thought.

"Incoming. They let loose with some sort of—"

The enormous explosion hit the back of the cave. They felt it even inside Alfa.

"Well, that was not very neighborly now, was it?" Cap said through clenched teeth.

They rushed to the bridge. First made a beeline for the control station, checked that all the weapons on top were online. She brought up the weapons selector. The enemy was still out of range, even for the emplacement on top of the mountain.

"Damn."

Cap was looking over her shoulder. "Nothing we can do, I'd rather not shoot and reveal the position of those emplacements if we don't have a chance at damaging them. They didn't hit them, so they probably haven't detected the defenses up there. What are they doing?"

"They are turning tail ... Why attack us like that and leave? They didn't even follow up, just a single shot and done." Noob was reading the data off the sensor station.

Cap turned to Ben. "Any ideas?"

"Don't look at me, I've no idea what makes these guys tick. I was here for a while and witnessed what they did to my crew, but I have no idea what they think."

Cap rubbed his chin. "This is very strange. Could it be they only had the one big missile?"

"They are gone. The long way around, they won't cross our field of fire."

Cap fell in the pilot chair. "Why would they ...?" he wondered out loud.

First got up. "I'll go to the back of the cave and take a look around. They may have breached it and we don't have sensors back there."

"Good idea. Take some and place them, just in case."

Noob got up too. "I'll go with you–"

"No, Noob, start the repairs. First can assist you when she gets back, but get the ball rolling. Ben, you stay by the sensors, I want eyes out there while First is placing the perimeter inside the cave. Come on, Noob, I'll help you out."

They each got started fulfilling their assignments.

FIRST WALKED UP TO the wall of the cave. The river head now split into two streams, one went out the mouth of the cave as before, however, the second one went through a new crack on the wall. A detailed inspection showed some loose rock.

She strained to pull some of the easily movable rocks in. There was a decent size hole, a lot of big chunks of jagged rock all around. Some easily weigh several tons, those were not moving, for sure. The whole mess seemed stable. She placed sensors and directional mines, just in case, then headed back.

"What's the verdict?" Asked Cap as she walked onto the bridge.

"They know we are here, they made a back door, they may be preparing for one of their sneak attacks."

Cap's eyes went over her and chuckled. "What did you do? Did you try to dig out?"

She looked down at herself and realized she was covered in wet white sand and rock powder. Gave a resigned shrug. "Hey, Cap? Since I'm already wet and all, how about I go out and scout the back? The river going out that way is about knee deep, but easily passable. I can set up a reception party for them, in case they decide to drop by. I don't think they'll be back any time soon. They tend to hit and run, and hide, before coming back."

Cap sat back and rotated the chair for a face-to-face. "You think it'll be useful? Or a good idea?" He sat forward placing his elbows on his knees and interlacing his fingers. "I'd hate to lose you."

First locked eyes with him. Then smiled. "Nothing like feeling wanted. I think we need to find out if we are vulnerable, I placed some mines and such, but on the inside, but by the time they activate, they'll be in the cave. I'll go out, set up a perimeter, and rush back."

Cap sat back. Nodded. "OK, but make it quick, I don't want you out and exposed if they decide to come back."

"Copy." She threw him an offhand salute and rushed out.

She didn't bother to change, she was going to get wet and filthy anyway. She loaded up on mines for the perimeter and passive sensors. She also added a shoulder holster beside the one on her hip. She checked the full charge on each blaster and the spare packs for each. She considered a carabine, but thinking back to the tight crawl space she was going to have to traverse made her decide against it. She did strap a wicked knife to her right calf.

On her way out she ran into Noob.

"You going out?"

"Just to set up a perimeter around the breach on the back. Out and in, quick and quiet."

"You be careful, OK? Be careful and quick, don't wander off."

She rolled her eyes, "Yes, mother."

The water cleared some of the sand from the fracture at the back. The exposed rock meant she could actually move through the opening hunched over easily, pulling the satchel behind her. The water was freezing cold already. It was an uncomfortable position, moving forward on her knees with water up halfway on her thigh, but it could be navigated without any major problems.

She was out. The sand all around her was blindingly white in the blazing sun, although the air was cool. She quickly set up a perimeter, both directional mines, and passive sensors.

Done, she stood up straight and turned to look around her, shading her eyes with her hand.

The water made its way into several meandering depressions, flowing freely away from the escarpment. She was curious. She looked back and bit her lower lip. Making up her mind, she jumped in the new stream, waist-deep in cool running water, and started moving downstream.

The water hid her heat signature. The aliens were sneaky, she was alert and ready for anything. Where could they be? She heard a noise to her left and froze. Underwater, her hand curled around the blaster in her hip holster. She didn't want to kill them, but she would if she had to.

This may not have been a good idea. She kept going, but after a while, she realized there was nothing new to see, just more desert in every direction.

Shaking her head for having done something as dumb as this she headed back.

As she approached the mountain, she came in behind an alien patrol. They were communicating with very low sounds, a language she didn't understand, but that alerted her to their presence before they realized she was right on top of them.

They knew of the river entrance, the attack was deliberate and purposeful, then. They were looking at it and seemed to be deciding if they should go in or not. They were far enough away that the perimeter she set up had not activated yet, on the other hand, Cap probably had them pegged by now.

She needed to communicate to those in the cave that she was OK, but if she used the comm she'd give herself away. This world was dead silent, any noise made it a long way.

She carefully retreated to the river and texted the ship underwater to muffle the sound, looking every which way, weary that she'll be attacked by the aliens any minute now.

The answer came. They will be ready at the river mouth. They tell her to circle around and come in from the front, they'll let her through, and the perimeter Friend/Foe recognition will be active and will protect her coming in.

She starts back, as quietly as possible.

Chapter 12

First ducked back down, quietly hiding in the shallow stream bed, pressing her back against the wet sand. The water was transparent, crystal clear, damn cold, and it did not offer any concealment.

That was the third alien patrol she'd seen. Frustration curled her fist tight and she resists the urge to bang the ground. Any sound would be a beacon in this silent world.

Ever so slowly, she crawled and glid on the water moving away from the aliens, making her moves echo those naturally made by the flowing stream.

Eventually, she peeked over the embankment. Finally, no one seemed to be around.

A glint to her right freezes her in place. She had missed the patrol. Now that she knew where to look, she made out the patrol slowly moving over a nearby dune. She froze and felt foolish. Her clothes, face, and hands, were caked with wet sand, so, from a distance, she may not be too noticeable. Movement, though, would betray her just as easily as color.

She waited patiently until the patrol crested the dune and slid behind, beyond her sight. A breath puffs out of her lips and she immediately regrets it. She must not make a sound.

First took her bearings. She had been advancing perpendicular to the course that would take her back to the cave and her friends. Frustrated, she inspected her surroundings.

A hulking dark shape in the distance caught her eye. The wreck.

As long as she doesn't turn the distress signal beacons off, the aliens would not be aware she was there. A shelter, of sorts. No food that she was aware of, but enough water nearby. Better than nothing. She started moving over to the wreck, keeping a wary eye in every direction at all times.

After what felt like a long time, she finally made it to the vicinity of the wreck and was happy to be inside out of the open desert.

She started to climb over the last dune between her and the wreck but stopped.

Approaching the ruined collection of ships carefully, crawling on her belly, she scouted the wreck. The aliens probably did not have a look-out all the time checking the immediate vicinity, they would have spotted it with the sensors in Alfa. She figured the trap must have some sort of proximity sensors that detected if anyone was near.

She calibrated the superb surveillance equipment Cap gave her. The readings showed why it was top of the line. She detected a passive sensor net, capable of sensing any approach and, she figured, reported the incident to the alien colony.

She made sure no stand-by transmission was going out and decided that, if she took it out all at once, it would not transmit at all and she'll be able to shelter in the wreck. The system seemed to have a single central transmitting hub, on the tallest part of the wreck. She took her blaster and sighted the hub. The red dot on her scope showed her where the bolt would hit. No way to be sure the device would be destroyed, but she had no other options open to her. One of the many advantages of the blaster, it was a quiet weapon. Not silent, but not loud either. She took the shot and waited for any sign of the aliens showing up. After quite a while there was no detectable activity, and she figured she had waited enough.

She ran a hand over her brow, caked with the fine white sand mixed with sweat, the air was not hot at all, but she exerted herself coming here. She inspected her immediate surroundings.

I've got to reach some inner area I can close off. The metal is dark on the outside, so the structure is probably warmer than the surrounding area if I find something to make fire with and if I'm deep enough inside, I'll be able to make a fire undetected. I need it, I'm freezing out in the open.

She checked her knapsack. Mostly tools for setting up the security perimeter, but she did find a sealed box with survival rations for a day. Two, with rationing. A smile slowly replaced her scowl.

"Cap, I will never, ever, argue with you again about what has to go in these deployment packs." She murmured.

She put it all in again and set off to explore the wreck.

She had a vague idea of the layout of the ruined cobbled-together ships, from the reports and video feed of Cap and Noob. Also, some of Ben's comments came to mind.

The outer areas were empty and looted. As she went deeper into the wreck, some rooms were in better shape. The occasional break in the hull allowed shafts of light to come in here and there. Those lit spots only helped to emphasize the cold darkness that engulfed her. She found a large compartment amidships, with solid walls and a working door. Working in the sense that was on hinges and she could close it, with a simple latch mechanism, no lock. She had gone deep into the wreck by now, no chance of light or sound making it out from here.

A long bench, with a few high chairs, and a pegboard ran all along one wall of the room. Evidently, this was a workshop of some sort. She examined her surroundings. Several heaps of parts run along the walls, about halfway up to the ceiling. Some parts seem newer than others.

She took out her comm.

"Alfa, this is First."

"About damn time. What took so long to report in? I was about to have Noob warm the ship up and go after the little bastards, they are all over the place, you know?"

She had to smile at Cap's breathless statement.

"Well, because the little bastards were all over the place I couldn't make my way back. I evaded as much as I could, but in the end, I had to come over to the wreck."

"We know." Noob's baritone sounded relieved. "We were tracking you on sensors. Good thing the aliens don't seem to have effective sensing gear, eh?"

That hadn't occurred to her. Well, she had been careful, but you couldn't hide from modern sensors. Not forever.

"I'm deep in the wreck. Some sort of workshop or something, I think. I don't see a single tool, but there are plenty of ... well parts, I guess." She said picking one up and dropping it. "Heaps of them."

"Listen," Cap interrupted her. "We'll keep an eye out for you, if the aliens make it over to your position, we'll give you a heads up. We'll proceed with repairs here and we'll figure out how to get to you."

"OK, but it's better if I come to you. We just have to make sure our hosts are not in my way."

"We'll see. First, you may have to shoot your way here or out of there. Do it with extreme prejudice. Take them out before they get a chance to shoot at you."

"I'm aware. Don't worry, if they come close, I'll find out just how much damage a blaster does to our hosts." She disliked having to think about killing these beings, she didn't like killing in general. These guys made it so she really was out of options, though, and if push came to shove ...

"Good, I want you to keep sharp, OK? Don't hesitate. If you are in trouble, shoot first, they have shown they don't care if they hurt us, so let's reciprocate."

"Yes, Cap, I said I would. Now go back to getting the ship fixed so we can leave this place."

"Take care, First." She was touched by the worry in Noob's voice.

"Copy. Out." She sat back on her haunches and looked around.

The oppressive darkness closed down on her. The welcome voices of friends had buoyed her spirits, but now she felt even more alone. The weak light of her flashlight illuminated the whole space, but the dancing shadows on the edge of her sight made her uneasy. Nothing flammable that she could see to make a fire. She rubbed her arms to infuse some warmth. She looked around the space.

"What are all these pieces?" She stood up and walked to the workbench along the wall. She put her knapsack there and took out an energy bar, opened it, and munched absentmindedly on it as she inspected the different pieces in the multiple heaps around her.

Chapter 13

First looked over the space she had taken over and concluded the best course of action was to check the rest of the wreck before settling down.

Quietly walking around inside the derelict, she found many different sections. She stayed towards the inner sections as much as possible, trying to avoid giving herself away in case there were patrols about. With time on her hands, she decided to take a closer look at the varied technologies present. Some, she identified quickly, others were alien, but had a certain familiarity, the rest were a complete mystery.

She found one of the strong rooms Ben told her about, a lot of jewelry for sure. Some metal bars she figured were precious to someone, too. She recognized gold, not just by its color, but because they were very heavy. She didn't recognize the stamp in bas relief or the language on them. Other ingots on shelves around the back wall she assumed were platinum, silver, and several she couldn't readily identify. They had not been disturbed and seemed to be just as they had been put away. Were the aliens not interested in such things? Did they have a completely different set of monetary value? Some of these metals were useful for industry, not just as commodities.

She kept looking. Some remains came from a robot ship, the design was cramped, unwelcoming to humans, and had heavily automated functions, with little if any areas for human interaction with the technology. After a little digging, she finally reached the memory core, although badly damaged, it was still accessible.

It was old. Thirty-five years old. She reactivated the core with Cap's equipment, read-only. This ship responded to a signal for help, following its program. Once in orbit around the planet, it transmitted a greeting to the wreck. The answer came in the form of a single missile that brought it down. The memory replay exhibited many gaps, but she pieced together what happened from the available information. She shook her head. These guys were not nice. She had to get this information to Cap. He had been right about not letting Beta come down. The aliens so far had ignored or not been able to target the *Einstein's Shadow*, but they had the capability of bringing down a ship from orbit. Or at least they had that capability thirty years ago or so.

Another portion of the wreck was a human vessel for sure. This one was from one of the many religious groups that traveled to the outer rim, looking for a virgin world where they could practice their religion in peace. They detected the call for help and came to investigate, according to the log. They were a colony ship. The written records she found in a diary indicated that the vessel had a full complement for colonization, therefore, the cargo was everything needed for terraforming an Earthlike planet. So, food might be available somewhere on this cold desolate rock. If the aliens found the food compatible with their physiology. If they didn't they might have simply disposed of it all. Many unknowns were still associated with the aliens. She moved on.

She kept looking and finding out what kinds of ships had fallen into the trap. She noted that no military ship had been trapped. Evening approached and she was hungry and tired. She walked out to a place where she could see out of the wreck and up at the stars. Time to call Alfa.

"We are a little busy here, our friends outside are getting ready to attack." Cap's answer was hurried, they were hustling over at the ship.

"How do you know?"

"Well, they didn't appreciate our closing of the river access, we blew the back entrance up and they, in turn, let loose with a couple of shouldered fired rocket-propelled grenades. The point defense system took them out, but they are setting up positions all around. They mean business, I think it's going to be a long night."

"It sure is. For you and me both."

"Here they come, talk to you later."

She heard the explosions and saw the sky light up over where the cave was. The howling frigid bitting wind masked some of the sounds. The battle started, the ending of it, the how of it, and the winner, like with all battles, was anyone's guess.

Tired, but resigned to not getting much if any rest, at least not right now, she went back into the wreck. Several areas were clearly 'bridges', she identified pilot stations, navigation stations, and sensor consoles.

The degree of ... looting? Destruction? Strip down? Whatever you would like to call it, varied from one area to the other. Some were stripped to the bulkheads, others had a lot of technology still in them. Other areas were barely touched. Whoever worked on the different areas was very inconsistent.

Satisfied that no one else was in the wreck, she went back to the area she had claimed. She considered going to the strong room, but it was an uncomfortable vault. Here she was reasonably safe, she could close the door if she needed to, and there were a couple of usable chairs, she didn't have to sit on the floor.

As she settled for the evening, she thought of her friends. The battle was going to be a tough one, for sure. Could she go out there and perform some sort of rear action? Could she distract the aliens? Could she ... Her fist came down hard on the bench. By herself, there were few options open to her to help them. She looked in their direction, although she couldn't see out of the windowless chamber. Her head hung in desperation and shame.

Chapter 14

The aliens had not taken kindly to Cap and Noob sealing the back opening their explosion made. A quick exploration of the rest of the cave confirmed the presence of thick solid unbreached rock walls all around. Also, they confirmed they were alone in the cave, it kept going deeper, but the sensors indicated it was a sealed pocket on the rock, and no tunnels were communicating anywhere. It was a deep cave, but a blind one. Now that they had sealed the river exit, there was only one way in. Alfa's cannons were there to welcome anyone foolish enough to try a frontal assault.

The shuttle's forward-facing weaponry was online and able to shoot in a two hundred and seventy degrees field of fire. Essentially, no frontal assault would succeed. They had set up an effective perimeter cover, with overlapping fields of fire, with three emplacements on top of the cave mouth to cover any approach from the flanks or the rear.

They supplemented the anti-personnel and anti-vehicle mines, they covered the whole area with passive sensors.

The aliens wouldn't be able to detect the sensors, but they'd be picked up immediately from quite a distance in any direction.

Cap, Noob, and Ben were sure they had covered every eventuality.

A great plan.

No plan, however, survives the first contact with the enemy.

"Alfa, this is First." Cap jumped in his seat and took a headset.

Noob pumped his fist in the air a few times.

"I knew she'd be OK." He murmured.

"But you were worried," Ben commented, still tagging the different approaching vehicles for the targeting system.

"Well, yeah, but I knew she'd be fine. She's tough, a good spacer. She wouldn't let these runts hurt her."

Ben heard Noob break in the conversation between First and the Captain and went back to his sensor readings.

"Incoming." Ben couldn't believe his voice sounded steady and not cracking, he trembled inside, but he was in control. "I read them painting the gun emplacements. I don't know what they are going to hit us with."

"Head in the game. Keep us appraised of anything they do, Ben. Noob, get ready, take out anything up-front, I'll coordinate the rest of the perimeter. Let's get this party started."

Cap walked over to Ben's side. "OK, they know we are here and that we are well-armed. No more love taps, they are coming in for the kill."

"I wish you didn't put it quite that way." Ben swallowed loudly; brushing sweat off his brow with a shaking hand.

Noob chuckled, "Life is tough. We are ready, time to teach them a lesson."

"They came at us with stealth the first couple of times, this time they are out in the open." Cap returned to his post. "They now know we are willing and able to fight. They will probably try to take us out for good, rather than—"

The aliens targeted their cave top units first. Several different missiles screamed towards the top of the cave, they were also shooting in the general direction with smaller weapons that were not in range, but the attackers shot anyway. They were unable to take the emplacements down, but the attack was intense. Several angry fire flowers blossomed in the air around their rocky refuge. The point defense system took many of the missiles out of the air before they were able to wreak havoc on their defenses.

The automatic systems were operating at capacity and the battle was engaged.

"Here they come. Straight at us. I read several different vehicles, and I mean different. The styles, the configuration, and even the power plants are different. I see a matched couple, about three are alike, but it's a mish-mash of models and sizes, all different."

Noob targeted oncoming vehicles with accurate fire, effectively stopping them in their tracks or destroying them if the armor gave way. "They are using tech salvaged from the captured ships. I'm guessing that's the most likely explanation."

Cap engaged the attackers coming at them from the flanks and the back. "I got a variety of targets over here too. They are more effective with some of the weapons than others, I have a feeling they are not used to fighting like this." He yelled the last part of his statement, even inside Alfa, the noise of the explosions becoming deafening.

A tremor went through the ship as a missile struck the side of the lip of the cavern, peppering the hull with rock fragments.

Ben screamed inarticulately at the rapping on the hull. "I'm going to die here in this barren, forsaken, sad, cursed rock."

"No, you are not, because I'm not." Noob kept his attention on the targeting system, intermittently shooting the advancing vehicles accurately. His body was tense, his movements measured and controlled.

"Nobody is dying, keep the sensor feed, and keep an eye out for air support," Cap commented cooly. He had been in this kind of situation before, in the war. They were outnumbered, but, so far, technology had given them the edge. Hopefully, they would keep the edge.

They kept at it for a long time. Cap was worried about First. They couldn't communicate until and if this was over, and then, only if they could make sure she was not in danger of being discovered, the aliens were not playing around. Could she be under attack right now? They were getting pummeled and they were dug in on an effective defensive posture. First was in a derelict, with just hand weapons against ... What?

Cap's thoughts were on the battle, but a part of him was still worried about what could be happening to First. Very worried.

Chapter 15

First had another energy bar and some water from her canteen. She looked around and paced the floor. Sat back down.

I really should try and sleep a little.

She propped up some tubes against the door. If opened, the sound would wake her. Not a great alarm system, but better than nothing. Laying down, she closed her eyes, crossed her arms, and tried to relax.

Well, that lasted a full five minutes.

She sat up and propped herself against the wall. It was useless. Worrying about what's going on at Alfa and what she's going to do next won't let her sleep.

She shook her head, got up, and dusted herself off.

I'm on my own and with no hope of rescue until the guys defeat the aliens. If they defeat the aliens.

She kicked some of the debris around her, the metallic, hollow sounds echoing in the mammoth, empty space. There was nothing she could do to help. Her head hung forward as she put her hands on her waist.

This is useless. She went out to keep investigating the wreck.

The aliens seemed to simply mash together whatever they didn't take away from the ships they captured. There was no rhyme or reason to the way the sections were put together. There were more strong rooms, filled with valuables. Whole computer or data processing rooms, all of them extensively vandalized, in different areas. Empty storage rooms. Abandoned and looted crew quarters. Some chambers had no purpose she could discern, the technology and distribution too alien to make an educated guess.

She came across a room full of discarded robots. The aliens had apparently taken what they needed and discarded the rest here from the different automatons.

With nothing better to do, she decided to take her time. Maybe she could find out something more, some more information. All the ships computer cores were gone or damaged, but maybe in this pile of refuse, there might be a memory core or two with useful information.

She cleared an area on the floor and started moving the different pieces from one side to the other, hoping she'll find something in usable shape in the immense pile of trash. There were a lot of discarded and destroyed robots. Everything from housekeeping, mechanic assistant, valet, and some which defied her attempts to determine their use or origin.

One of the robot's designs was human and seemed in reasonable shape, compared to the rest of the pile. The body was badly battered, dented, burnt, and scraped, but the logic and memory cores were intact. There were no limbs or means of propulsion, she couldn't tell if originally arms or legs were attached to the body, or if it moved on caterpillar threads, but the central carapace had been discarded with all the 'thinking' parts of the robot intact inside, a mistake, perhaps, the aliens might have taken the head, thinking these components were there. The scorch marks around the top of the body and the jagged edges suggested a more violent removal process of the head, though.

She repurposed a power source from another robot, speakers from another, a sensor suite from yet another, and so on. Finally, she had a Frankenstein-ish amalgamation of equipment. After some further tweaking, it responded.

"Unit 2812. Marginally on-line. Unable to run a complete diagnostic. Extensive null responses."

"I hooked you up with a sensor suite. Can you detect your environment?" First realized that if the microphone was not working, it wouldn't even know she asked the question. She had done everything right, as much as she could, it should be OK, but she couldn't know if—

"Sensor suite online. Not optimal equipment. Subnormal response time and coupling."

She smiled. "Stop bellyaching, it's the best I could do with what I had."

"I don't have a belly and I don't ache. That is a nonsensical command."

Literal much? Interesting statement, though.

"Report last recorded memories."

The response was slow and rendered in a scratchy ... voice?

"Under attack, ship: damaged beyond repair, crew: captured, internal equipment and supplemental complement: destroyed or vandalized."

"What happened to the captured crew?" This sounded eerily like Ben's story.

"Some of the crew were taken from the ship as prisoners. Others were consumed in the ship."

"Taken as prisoners ... Wait. What? What do you mean consumed?" She stood up from the overturned bucket she had been sitting on, her hands curling into fists.

"The attackers consumed the crew's bodies. Mostly the ones who had expired. Some who were very badly wounded. Those wounded were consumed first."

First struggled to find her voice. Sitting back on her haunches, she rocked back and eventually sat on the floor, her mouth hanging open.

No. No intelligent star-faring species ate other intelligent star-faring species. It just didn't happen. Ever.

Chapter 16

The night was lit with explosions and tracer rounds. The aliens used them to guide their fire, but it was all for nothing. Tracers were a good way to follow the trajectory of their ammo and fine-tune their aim, but it also allowed Cap and Noob to see where the fire originated from. The crew of Alpha had used this to devastating effect.

The relentless and vicious attack came from all sides. A couple of times some elements of the alien force made it to the vicinity of the cave, on both flanks. The front was effectively defended by Alfa's fire. The rear had a large kill zone from the top mounted weapons. The sides seemed to be a way to try and flank them, ideally to then engage in close combat. The perimeter mines took a devastating toll on the forward attackers. The remaining alien attack force picked up their few wounded and retreated. They left their dead behind.

The automatic guns on top of their defense perimeter were autonomous out of necessity. There was no way to supplement their ammo, once they engaged in battle. Cap's virtuoso performance was epic. Each gun could be targeted independently, his attentive guidance prevented the aliens from finding any chinks in the armor. Their rear was littered with bullet-riddled bodies and damaged or destroyed equipment.

Noob's fire was devastating to the incoming vehicles. Regular ammunition, they decided earlier to use straight ammunition, not incendiary or armor-piercing, but it was superbly effective against the incoming enemy.

The sun was starting to rise over the horizon when Ben turned to the others, his eyes bloodshot from staring intensely at the sensors all night. "They are breaking off." A wild whoop escaped from him as his left fist pumped the air.

Noob's shirt was sticking to his back, sweat rolled freely down his sides. "I'm glad they decided to leave, I'm almost out of the large-caliber rounds. I thought I'd have to go down and switch to the specialty ammo."

Cap relaxed on his chair too, sitting back away from the console. He wiped his brow. "I'm glad they broke off. We'll have to swap out the weapons on top of the cave. The ammo there is almost gone too. Fifteen, maybe twenty minutes more, and the guns would have gone dry."

"And then what? We're vulnerable?" Ben's face went pale, a tremor making its way into his voice. His shoulders slumped.

Noob let out a laugh. "No, Ben, we'll switch to energy weapons. We have plenty of energy, no problem, now that we've made repairs. We still can fight back. Alfa's got a mean bite. That's why we came down in her." He said patting the console in front of him.

"OK, people, let's get going, they did score a few hits. Let's fix something to eat and drink and we'll start repairs. Noob, you catch some sleep after breakfast. I'll stay up with Ben and work on Alfa. When you get up, I'll go up top, swap the damaged guns and reload the others. Ben can catch a few hours of sleep at that time. I'll rest when I come back."

"Yes, sir."

As Noob and Ben left the bridge, Cap turned to the transmitter. He put out a multidirectional signal: "First do not respond. They are breaking off and presumably going back to their cave, to hide and lick their wounds. They are not moving in your direction, but we don't know if they'll change trajectory. Do not engage if they run into you. This is a significant force and they are not playing around." The bit about their route was nonsense. Some alien elements would pass the wreck on their way back to their spider hole, but the more confusion the better. If they could intercept and understand the message, Cap wanted them to be disoriented as much as possible. Satisfied that even if they intercepted the transmission, they would not know where to find her, he went back to the galley.

It was a long day of hard work. They finished as many repairs to the damaged weapons emplacements as they could. Outside, they supplemented the areas of the defense perimeter which were activated or destroyed.

The grisly chore of moving the aliens' remains where necessary took its toll on all of them. They needed to check they were all in fact dead and none were just playing possum, in order to stage a sneak attack. A few aliens were badly hurt and died before they could get to them safely. None of the aliens left behind were alive by the time they got to them.

It wasn't until sunset that they were in any shape to think about getting in touch with First again.

Chapter 17

First salvaged some more equipment to complement what she adapted to the robot, trying to bring it to an acceptable level of performance. Rocking back on her heels, she squatted next to its lower half, screwdriver in hand looking at her handiwork, the robot was almost up and running.

Now ambulatory, the robot could move slowly on two independent wide single tracks. A single manipulator, unfortunately. On the one hand, because she only found one of adequate size, there were others, but they would most likely not fit. On the other hand, because it was the only compatible driver for that kind of peripheral she found. None of the other available equipment interfaced adequately to be incorporated by the robot. The robot's existing programs would not operate any of the few other arms she found. Many more advanced, versatile, and better appendages were available all around, but the drivers which would allow the robot to control them were unavailable, so, a stumpy two-legged, one-armed robot resulted from her efforts. The sensory array was exposed, not housed in a clear or colored dome, on a swiveling base, with exposed servos. The speaker was also exposed and produced a scratchy but marginally adequate voice. Noisy. Ugly too.

Once she brought 2812 fully online, the robot helped her explore the remains of the unit's original ship. She found some lockers with tools and a few work clothes that had not been completely looted as well as some areas with available power. She had the robot charge while the battle was going on.

"As soon as the fight over there ends, you disconnect and close everything down. I don't want any signals going out by chance."

"I detect a repeating signal going out. Heavily garbled but appears to be an emergency cry for help, a distress signal of some sort."

"Yes, leave that one."

"It lured my ship here. We should disconnect it, appears to be the bait for a trap."

"It is a trap. If we disconnect the emitter, the aliens will realize something is up here and they'll come to find out what happened to their lure. They'll take me, at the very least, and disassemble you, so, let's leave it be, for now, OK?"

"It's sound reasoning. I'll allow it. Let's leave the signal active, for now."

She had to laugh. The dry-clipped way the robot talked was amusing sometimes.

"So tell me more. What happened to the crew they took? Did any of them ever come back?"

"No. The unknown life forms came back. They stripped the equipment down to the bulkheads. They also took some of the internal paneling and all the fuel. They used some of the automated units, those they interfaced with easily. All others were ... disposed of."

"So you were uncooperative."

"In the extreme. As far as I was able to, which wasn't much, I'm afraid. I am a battle droid. I was being delivered to an intelligence unit at a military camp in a colony near the rim. I was packed and stored in the forward hold. They brought me out but did not remove the security seals. I was active but had a governor on, so I was immobile at the onset of the action. I detected activity, what was happening around me, but I was incapacitated."

"Why?"

"Regular precaution when transporting battle droids destined to a hot zone. We are unable to move until we reach the destination and are deemed fit for duty. There has never been a malfunction of a battle droid in a ship, as far as I'm aware, but I can see how the event would be quite unfortunate. We are superb battle machines. I also have an intelligence package, so my model is even superior to the regular battle bots"

"So they came in and found you and took you apart?"

"Not quite. One of the officers came in and removed the governor, turned, and fled. I understood at the time he wanted me to buy him time to escape. He was badly injured in his escape attempt almost immediately, though. He was consumed soon after. I came fully online but had no ammunition. My power weapons were off-line until we reached our destination, another safety precaution, so I had to fight hand to hand."

She was sitting on her hunches and listening to the heap of scrap tell her of a battle droid who fought the aliens they were facing hand to hand. "So, what happened?"

"I proceeded with a frontal attack on the enemy. There was no need or opportunity for stealth. They knew I was on the ship and my function. We engaged and I was successful in bringing down a few of them before their superior numbers and fire-power took me down."

"What's a few?"

"I took down, dead or gravely injured, close to 75 hostiles. Several hostiles suffered minor injuries, but I was unable to determine the extent of the inflicted damage or the number of hostiles taken off the line, or if they would be able to recover. The wounds appeared to be enough to cause them to slow down and resulted in profuse bleeding, but given that I do not have files on their physiology or anatomy, I was unable to determine the severity, amount, or degree of damage."

"Well, then how can you tell the 75 you mentioned before were gravely injured?" She said with a smile. "Wait a sec, I've got an incoming message."

She read the text from Cap from a multidirectional signal, the aliens were retreating. She turned her attention back to the robot.

"Dismemberment is usually enough to take a fighter out of combat for a prolonged period of time. Most of the injuries were of that sort." Her jaw dropped. "The ones I was sure were dead, about 60, had enough body injuries that I am certain they could not be brought back."

"I'm surprised they didn't fry you then."

"So was I. They did proceed to dismember me, my appendages were blown off with repeated concentrated fire from several different weapons, and their projectile weapons dented my external armor and made it difficult for me to advance. The main sensor array on top of my body was heavily damaged shortly after, the dome and most of my armor were shot off. From that point on my information gathering capabilities suffered in quality and quantity."

"After they blew your head off? Yes, I would say that would do it."

"The events I recorded later were ... unlikely. At least they seemed so to me."

That picked her interest. "Why? What happened? What do you think happened?"

"I don't think as such. My interpretation of the sensory impressions recorded must be wrong. I concluded from the available input they ate their dead."

"WHAT?"

"I concluded from the—"

"I heard you the first time." She was up and panting. Cannibals? Cannibals! It could not be. No known intelligent species were cannibalistic. Not one. Some indulged in the practice in the distant past, but not now, not in the era of space travel. No, it could not be. It was bad enough thinking they could consume other sentient species but, to eat their own? That was unthinkable.

2812 was quiet for a while. Patiently waiting for her to say something.

"We have to tell the others."

"That will have to wait. The aliens are here."

Now knowing the aliens might not just try to capture her, but actually might try to eat her, First decided if it came to a fight, it would be to the death. She would not be captured. No way.

Chapter 18

First crouched into a fighting stance, ready for anything. She looked around frantically and reached for her blaster.

"Where? Where exactly are the aliens? How many?" She was panting and looking around, even though this deep in the wreck, she couldn't see outside.

"They are passing us about a mile away."

Relief flowed like cool water over her. "How do you know? Are you using passive sensors?"

"It's not difficult to pick them up. They are using rather loud motorized vehicles. You can probably perceive them too. The currently installed sensor suite is precarious at best, but adequate enough for my rough estimation of their location."

The eerie quiet soon gave way to a distant rumbling. The alien vehicles. They were clunky and loud, for her to be able to hear them all the way in here. She looked frantically around, but everything was off, except for the robot.

"2812 shut down—"

"All equipment that might broadcast any signal has been shut down or disengaged. They will not pick me up. I found no detectable signal emissions, aside from the emergency beacon and a locator buoy."

The buoy! She truly hoped they didn't pick this time to come and take the damn thing away. What was it Ben said? They deactivated the one they left. To draw more victims in, obviously. They hadn't had time yet? Were they trying to take them down first? Limiting the number of opponents on the ground? Such a strategy would make sense and would be in line with what she knew of the aliens.

She was tempted to go out and disengage the signal, but only for a second. If the aliens were indeed monitoring the buoy and it stopped broadcasting, they might decide to come and check why, and they'd find lunch. A shudder went through her.

She leaned back against the wall and let herself slide down until she was sitting on the floor.

"I would move over and offer some support or comfort, but I'm afraid it may generate some noise and or unintended signals."

"That's OK. Stay put. They should be past us in a relatively short time."

However, it took a good long time for the aliens to pass. There were a lot more vehicles than she had initially estimated, or were new ones incorporating into the passing column? Where were those coming from?

Chapter 19

First had an energy bar and the last of her water. "I'm going to have to go out and gather water soon."

"That would be inadvisable at this time. At least not until we have some information regarding the location of the enemy." 2812 stated, matter of factly. "It's one of the many limitations organics have, that dependence on constant hydration and nourishment."

A small smile danced on First's lips for a second, then her forehead furrowed in a deep frown. "Listen, you bucket of bolts, you are no better. You need energy and ... and ... well, you in particular need ammo, so don't give me that crap." She'd had few interactions with robots in general. They were common enough, but they performed their tasks and that was literally that. She had never been in a situation like this, or with a robot of this caliber and complexity before.

"The needs of a sophisticated automated unit such as myself, when properly maintained and cared for, are much less than that of organic beings."

She was amused, but also a little concerned at the superior attitude of the robot. "When maintained and cared for by us lowly organic beings, so watch your mouth, you are bearly functional thanks to me, I don't buy your superior attitude."

"Typical denial of reality. That too is a common limitation of—"

"First, do you copy?" Cap's voice. Loud and clear from her comm.

"Right here." She shook her head, glad for the interruption.

"Time for you to head out, we detect no alien guards posted, all sensor sweeps are clear."

"OK, I'm bringing a robot with me, I think you'll be interested in what it has to say in terms of what he witnessed. As for the robot itself, let's say that his personality is an acquired taste, and I haven't acquired it just yet."

Cap's full belly laugh came loud and clear. "I can't believe you let a piece of machinery get under your skin."

"Wait 'till you meet it. All milk and honey, I'm telling you. We are on our way." She closed the comm. "You think you'll be fine?"

"The repairs are adequate, if not satisfactory. I'm ambulatory, after a fashion, and I believe the caterpillar tracks will actually aid in traversing the sandy soil. So, yes, I'll be fine."

"You are not one for economy of words, are you?"

"I am sure I don't know what you mean by that."

"Exactly," First said chuckling and rolling her eyes. She gathered her few belongings, loaded up 2812 with a few things she figured they'd need ... and some jewels and ingots, since the vault was on the way out, and headed for Alfa.

THE OUTER HATCH OPENED welcoming them home. At least for First, it's literally a warm homecoming feeling after spending time deep in the frigid belly of the wreck. Not quite as cold as it would have been out, exposed to the elements, but a trying experience all the same.

"Hi, I'm home." She called out as the outer hatch closed.

"Come up to the bridge, we are all here," Cap instructed them over ship-wide. Cap, Noob, and Ben covered them on their trek, both with passive and active sensor sweeps, and manning the guns. Ready for anything. They stayed on the sensors since the aliens had a knack for showing up unexpectedly.

2812 rolled ungainly onto the bridge and stopped short. First bumped into it as she rushed forward to her shipmates. "What's the matter with you?" First bent to rub her shins, which she banged pretty good on 2812.

"Sir. Colonel Skerrit. I'm 2812, able combat unit, currently not in optimal condition. Evidently, I have seen better days, not at my best at the moment. Your officer was able to restore some of my systems. My present amalgamated self is quite useless, but if the armory is available, I could try to assemble something."

Noob and Ben looked at First, who shrugged and frowned in confusion. They all turned to Cap.

Cap gave a deep sigh and leaned back on the pilot's chair. "How far back do your records go? I would have thought no one would recognize me anymore."

"I was given information on all on and off-duty forces, but details only on officers of the upper echelons. Military Intelligence officers in the deployment area were included as a matter of course. In the event the situation was fluid and command had to be transferred quickly. Our being able to identify the command line would expedite the process."

"OK, go in the back, see what you can get, and select it, but do not incorporate it until authorized. This is not a military transport or a military operation. We may need the components for something else."

"Yes Sir."

"Cap. Just call me Cap."

"Yes Sir, your denomination has been changed to Cap, when in public."

Cap rolled his eyes, "Military Intelligence is indeed an oxymoron, exhibit A," he sighed, pointing at 2812

"My initial assessment was an undercover military crew on a covert operation. Cap, you may want to limit the knowledge of my function. Since there are civilians here."

"Indeed there are, 2812, indeed there are."

"Military Intelligence? Cap, we need to talk." First finally made it all the way onto the bridge stepping around the robot and patting greeting everyone.

"We do. Indeed, we do. But we have to eat and rest, so let's take care of that now."

They went to the galley and settled down. Everyone was wondering what was up with Cap. First knew him best of all, and she knew he was a veteran, but a Coronel? What the heck?

Chapter 20

During the meal, First recounted her experience in the wreck and told them about what she brought back with her. Especially the jewelry and precious metals, which she had stowed in the hold upon coming in. They were all happy to have her back. Even Ben was caught up in the moment, although he was a newcomer to the group.

All through the meal and the banter, First couldn't shake the surprise of Cap's rank. She trusted he'd tell her when the time was right.

"First, come with me, let's get 2812 all squared away."

"Yes, Cap." She got up to follow him and to talk in private.

As they walked toward the war chest, their substitute for an armory, First decided to breach the subject. "Um, Cap? None of my business, of course. You've been good to me for many years and all, and I ..." she dried her hands on her pants as they walked.

"What is it? Spit it out, First. It's not like you to beat around the bushes."

"Must be rubbing off on me from the 'bot. Well, Colonel? You? I mean, I knew you were a veteran, I was an officer in the University Reserves, as you are aware, served for a while per contract. I put it all in my resume, I saw a little action, not much. I didn't know you were an officer. Not that high up."

A smile played with the corners of Cap's lips. "Well, then I haven't lost my touch. I was regular army, then I worked intelligence for some time at the end of my stint, but decided to quit. The war was unpleasant, many nasty things needed doing and got done."

He got serious and seemed a little sad too. " After it was all over, I felt I didn't want to be in the service anymore. I had saved a little money, so ..." He looked around as if he could see beyond the walls of the passageway to the rest of the ship. "I decided to buy myself a rig, a massive one, so the trips would be between stars, and put some distance from everything for years at a time. It was part of my cover in intelligence, being an interstellar hauler, so I knew the life. I had the contacts, so the transition was not hard or long. And it worked too. Nice people on the crew, I always make sure I got a competent crew, and, well, the rest I think you know."

She nodded. She still had a difficult time picturing Cap as one of those steely-eyed, ramrod straight back, hyper-serious career military types. He was strict and sometimes severe, sure, but a regular guy most of the time. She shook her head, baffled.

They assembled as much of a body as they were able to for 2812, the caterpillar tracks stayed on, but two adequate manipulators and a proper sensor suite completed the robot.

As they worked, First lowered her voice. "Cap, there is something I think we should discuss and, er, keep between us for now, at least."

"What is it?" Cap asked, concentrating on attaching the manipulators and making all the correct connections.

"2812 gave me some rather unwelcomed news while I was with him in the wreck." She proceeded to tell Cap all about the aliens eating their captives and some of their own.

Cap stopped what he was doing and turned to her. "Did you get any evidence aside from the report from the 'bot?"

"No."

"2812, give me a concise report on the aliens' behaviors after the battle."

2812 went over it all again. This time with even more gruesome details. He was also a lot more precise in terms of the timing of the battles and the way the aliens deployed once on board. Cap simply took it all in as he and First worked on the unit.

The unit was now much more presentable. The battle components were not available, not even in the deep locked lockers of Cap.

"I have some components that might work for you on the *Einstein's Shadow*, but not here. Sorry."

"No need to be sorry, Cap. I'm mobile and able to collaborate, so I am operational. I would like to supplement my offensive capacity, and I'll be as ready as viable."

Cap gave his permission and 2812 went to load up on as many offensive weapons as he could use. There will be a need for the robot to use them sooner rather than later.

Chapter 21

"Cap, I got news for you, but you are not going to like them."

"Let me have them, Gears, don't give the comments, just give me the news." Cap rubbed his forehead, they were low on ammo, the energy weapons were OK and he thought they could probably keep the aliens at bay with them, but...

"You may not be reading this yet, because the activity is on the far side from you but, you know the mountain the aliens have the large hatch at? The one you explored?"

"Yes? What about it? What's going on?"

They had rested, at least four hours of sleep each, which was adequate, if not necessarily enough. Most of the essential repairs were done, they only needed a couple of more things, and they'd be able to go.

First and Noob got up from their consoles and dashed over to Cap's side. Their hurried steps were a clear sign of their anxiety. They had gone over everything and had a very clear idea of what their situation was. The situation, as such, wasn't sustainable for long.

Ben still slept in the back.

"We got a small spike, we would have missed the activity, but we have kept that mountain under close observation for this very kind of event."

"Gears, I swear, get to the point." Cap's exasperation was clear in his voice.

"There is a hangar door opening up. I mean a hangar door, Alfa could fit through easily, maybe with Beta and Gamma on top. This opening is enormous."

Cap's forehead creased with deep furrows. Not welcomed news, that's for sure. "Is anything coming out?"

"Not yet, but we are reading a lot of activity there."

First moved to the sensor suite. "I'm reading the activity now too. Wow, they are emitting a lot of energy, they have something big warming up."

"Not helping, First."

"Sorry, Cap. I'll keep an eye on it."

"I don't like this. We are too far to call for help from Mobula 3. If that is a space-worthy ship, the *Einstein's Shadow* may have to hot-foot it out of the system."

"What about us?!" Ben screamed, coming from the entrance to the bridge where he stood quietly until now. "I thought you guys would rescue me, but if the star-ship takes off, we'll be stuck and we won't survive. The aliens will... take us. Take us all."

"Yeah, about that. 2812 tells some shocking stories about the aliens, which you have neglected to share. Why is that?" First asked Ben, turning to face him and folding her arms.

"What stories? What are you talking about?"

"2812 told us of the aliens eating the prisoners, and even some of their own." First deadpans the delivery, looking intently at Ben for any reaction.

Ben's face lost all color. His mouth opened a couple of times, but only the smallest of whimpers were audible. His eyes rolled back on his head and he fell forward towards the deck.

Noob rushed forward and caught him before he hit the floor. "I have a feeling he wasn't aware of that little tidbit."

"You think?" First turned back to her console as Noob placed Ben in the supernumerary chair at the back and strapped him in, just in case.

"We are reading ground vehicles exiting the hangar door. Nothing airborne, but, guys, there are a lot of them." Gears' tone was somber.

"I read them." First hands were all over the console. "Heavy vehicles, some with threads, some with tires, all surface vehicles as far as I can tell, and they are all coming for us."

Cap read the ammo counts one more time. They were still the same numbers, pathetically low.

First continued her report. "They are coming straight at us, in a single lump. I can't make out a coherent formation of any sort or any order, a disorganized mob of vehicles." She turned to Cap. "There are a lot of them, Cap, they appear heavily armed."

"We can't hold out against that." Noob's comment was a whisper, but they all heard it.

They had only a couple of hours before the enemy column reached their position. How could they possibly defend against the sizable force bearing down on them?

Cap was thoughtful for a moment, then turned to First. The exchanged glance was enough. They were outgunned.

Chapter 22

Cap got up and headed for the back. His crew was solid, trustworthy people, all of them. He wanted to save them if he could. He was going to damn well try his best.

"First, with me. Noob, keep an eye on our friends over there and keep us up to date with the estimated arrival, give us five-minute intervals."

"You got it." Noob said as he took First's place at the sensor suite.

Beyond the war chest, Cap opened a locker deep in Alfas cargo hold.

"First? Bring the cart, we are going to need it." He said through clenched teeth, all his muscles taught, lifting a box of high yield anti-vehicle mines from the locker, a couple of smaller antipersonnel mine boxes under it clearly visible now.

"You have those many mines? Exactly what else do you have in Alpha? For that matter, what do you have in Beta and Gamma?"

"I like to be prepared." Cap smiled back at her.

"Prepared is one thing, this is amazing."

Outside, they split up, covering as much ground as they could, placing the mines in the likely routes of approach. They prepared to receive the aliens and fortify the battle line as much as they could.

"That's the last of the ammo, Cap. Shouldn't we save some, just in case?"

"No, it's better to run out of ammo than to look like we are running out of ammo. We need to give them a bloody nose, hard enough that they decide we are not worth pursuing."

"You know they are not going to let us go, right? They can't risk our getting out of here and letting the Colonial Authority find out about their trap."

"You might be overthinking it, First. They have caught other species, they may not care or may not even be aware there is such a thing as the Colonial Authority."

"I hope you are right."

"We've hardened the target as much as we can. We have to take any chance we get and leave now. We'll have to do without some of the little repairs still pending."

"We've tried that before, we have been shot down every single time." First finished picking up after them and headed to the hatch.

"Yes, but I suspect this is an all-out push by the aliens. If we make it, we'll have a window in which we'll be able to leave." Cap walked with her, carrying the rest of the material they were not going to leave out.

2812 got ready to assist with fire control and manned the top rear gun emplacements.

Ben was up when they made their way back to the bridge. Still wobbly and wild-eyed, he seemed to somewhat have come to grips with the latest grisly news.

"Let's get ready, folks." Cap moved over to look over Noob's shoulder.

"Cap, I don't think you should let the robot control those guns. We don't know anything about it." Ben's trembling voice showed clearly he still wasn't fully recovered or thinking straight.

"I can be authenticated easily. The Colonel can also vouch for me, my identifying him speaks in my favor."

"I ... I don't see it that way. You've been here a long time, how do we know they haven't messed with you?" His eyes lit up. "Hey! You are a battle robot, right? So, go out, fight them outside, that'll give us a better chance."

"The kind of assault they will be performing precludes my surviving close contact of the kind you suggest. I will be much better used here, manning gun emplacements remotely."

"Your survival doesn't matter, you are supposed to be used to protect soldiers and civilian lives, so, you should be willing, eager in fact, to go out and face off with those aliens."

"I take exception to your pointing out my survival doesn't matter. It matters to me, I do have self-preservation routines."

"It's irrelevant if it matters to you or not, you are a machine, and you will obey the orders given to you." Hollered Ben.

"Enough." Cap thundered over the argument. "We can use him in here if the outer defense perimeter is breached. Outside, on the other hand, they might pick him off from a distance. He stays in here with us."

"How do you know we can trust it? How do you know–"

"Ben. Shut up." Noob's tone did not invite an answer.

"Final check, Make sure everything is loaded and online. This is going to be nasty." Cap's firm voice helped them all get a grip.

They each concentrated on the consoles in front of them. First rechecked the battery charge levels and made sure the generator was ready to supplement the load. Noob's hands stopped every so often to ball up in fists while he tested the targeting mechanisms. 2812 interphased with the remote control of the emplacements, the flashing notifications on the screens too quick for the eye to follow.

Everyone reported defenses set up and ready.

"Cap, we can send Gamma on auto, you or First can pilot it remotely and use the shuttle as air cover." Gears swallowing came through the comm loud and clear. "Cap, a lot of them are coming your way, heavy vehicles. I can't read enough details from here, but they seem to have a lot of heavy weapons. I think you might want additional support."

Cap sat back on his chair. Deep in thought for a full minute. The play of emotions on his face made plain that he was giving the suggestion serious consideration.

"Cap?"

"No, Gears. I ran the numbers in my head just now, Gamma would not make it here in time to make a difference. Besides, it's not worth losing another shuttle if we can't make it out."

Two bright pink spots blossomed on Ben's pale cheeks. His eyes wide, he asked in a small voice. "Are we going to die?"

"Not if we can help it. Keep it together. We'll be alright."

Ben turned to First to thank her for the encouragement and took in the beads of sweat on her forehead, the dampness visible under her arms. He gulped and turned around trying to focus on what everyone is doing.

Noob lifted his eyes from his fire station. "Ben, man your station and get your head in the game."

2812's unemotional voice butted in. "Guys, hate to break up your argument, but company is here."

Chapter 23

A savage all-out attack by the aliens. No quarter asked, no quarter given.

The alien's ferocious attack started with peppering their position with long-range weapons. Heavy slugs of some metal or another rained on their rocky shelter, the fire was intense but not very accurate. The thunder of explosions all around reached them even as sheltered as they were. The frontal view was obscured by the billowing clouds of white sand the explosions threw up in the air. The lead vehicles were still out of range of Alfa's weapons, so there was nothing to do but endure the onslaught.

The wave of vehicles spread out as they approach at breakneck speeds, forming a wide semicircle advancing towards Alpha's position. The aliens kept up a high volume of fire, now some smaller weapons were getting in the fight.

"Almost in range." First's voice was firm, but indifferent, though, cold even.

"As soon as they are in range, fire at will, but fire for effect only, no suppressing fire, we don't have the ammo for that."

"Copy." Noob, First, and 2812 all answered in unison.

"Got it." Called out Ben, half a second later.

"Almost there ... keep coming." Muttered Cap.

The first explosions from the anti-vehicle mines placed earlier in the expected insertion routes broke the line of vehicles coming their way. Most of the alien shots lost any accuracy and, in fact, quite a few of the advancing vehicles ceased their fire altogether. Some of the vehicles not affected by the explosions veered from their path and careered into the adjacent one in the formation. The minefield was quite effective in breaking up the frontal attack.

Amid all the carnage on the front assault line, a rear action took place. A phalange of armed aliens came up against the positions controlled by 2812. All infantry, no vehicles in support. 2812s fire was accurate and devastating. The sheer number and ferocity of the aliens were effective weapons in themselves. They were relentless in their attack and even though they suffered terrible losses, they targeted each emplacement repeatedly.

The enemy overwhelmed 2812s positions eventually. There were simply too many aliens, 2812 took a lot of them out of the fight, most permanently. By the sheer magnitude of the attack, they prevailed, reaching the peripheral layer.

2812 followed their advance and waited patiently. Most of the guns were out of the fight, either dry or damaged. The rest were silent, playing dead as it were.

The lull in fire emboldened the aliens to surge forward and attempt to climb their mound from the back. As they approached recklessly, under the vigilant scrutiny of 2812, they met a tightly packed antipersonnel minefield laid earlier by Cap and First. Their line incredibly absorbed the losses, regrouped, and started towards the back of Alpha's shelter once again.

"Down to my last guns, Colonel, correction, Cap. They have breached the outer perimeter and are now advancing on the top position. They are gaining, I will set guns in auto fire and proceed to go up top and engage in hand-to-hand combat, when necessary. Unfortunately, I'm poorly equipped. Nobody's fault, just stating a fact." 2812 started towards the back and out of Alfa.

"Did that robot just reprimand us?" First asked, amused.

"I have a feeling there is more to that robot than we know. Might be a good idea to keep it, if we make it out of here." Said Cap while concentrating on his console.

"You know I can still hear you, right?" Came 2812's synthetic voice from the speakers.

"I'm telling you, this robot is weird," Ben said with a shudder.

Cap shrugged, "It's different, that's for sure."

A few minutes go by, and the last of the guns top side goes quiet, the clash audible over the communicator. 2812 engaged the aliens.

The frontal assault had several clear gaps. No longer coordinated and down by a good fifty percent, the crew can concentrate on each of their targets. It was immediately apparent that the approaching vehicles were from very different styles and designs.

"Clearly, they are all scavenged. I like these aliens less and less as time goes by." Noob stated as he sighted his targets.

"Yeah, well, let's show them what we think of them, right?" First had her targets in her sights.

The lead vehicles were now far ahead of the others. All discipline lost, and every driver went as fast as the vehicle would allow.

The incoming fire had so far not been accurate, scoring many times on the cave walls, but none on Alfa. Not yet, and First wanted to keep it that way. She waited until her fire control indicated a solid fix on the approaching vehicles. The middle of the advancing formation was her area of responsibility. Her sights were on a large heavily armored eight or ten wide-wheeled vehicle with a cannon that coughed artillery shells with depressing regularity. She could make out the slits the aliens used to look out in the armor on her sights. Her guns loaded with regular ammunition, for now, she had to make her shots count. She targeted the general area of the lookout slits, hoping for a soft spot or a lucky shot. She let fly, controlled short bursts. Three, six, then nine impacts before one made it in. The hulking vehicle lost control and drunkenly smashed into the lighter armored one next to it. She continued to fire, short, accurate, devastating bursts, taking out vehicle after vehicle.

Cap and Noob were shooting seconds apart, raining destruction down on their targets.

The road to the cave's mouth was now littered with broken down and burning vehicles, the smoke thick and dark, staining the sky. The white sand punctuated everywhere with maroon blood, soot, and the different large burning husks of the defeated vehicles.

Less than five vehicles remain active, now easy targets since they were the only ones advancing on their position. They were quickly and effectively taken out.

The surviving aliens had been coming out of the overturned and blown-up vehicles and broke into two groups. The smaller of the two gathered their wounded and started back to their lair. The bigger one started moving towards Alfa in a savage frontal attack.

They ran into the antipersonnel minefield and, incredibly, this didn't stop or slow them down.

"These guys have lost their mind. That's a suicide run." Cried out Ben.

Ben and Noob were each covering their fields of fire. Trying to score a hit with every projectile.

Cap kept his eyes on his targeting console. "Single shots. Let's make it last. Keep them busy and hurting, but single shots!"

The guns went dry.

They had no more ammo, they switched to energy weapons immediately, but they knew they would overheat soon in a prolonged attack.

The aliens were down to a small group. Small in the sense that many had fallen, but there were still at least seventy more aliens out there, coming at them, and nobody had any doubts about their intentions.

The aliens now had plenty of places to take cover with the numerous vehicles disabled on the field of battle. They kept a steady offensive. Rocket-propelled grenades, small shoulder-launched missiles, they threw a lot of ordinance at Alpha.

They targeted and defeated every threat, but the toll on the energy weapons was substantial.

"That's it, we are dry." Called out First when the last of the energy weapons reported overheating and shut down.

"Time to meet the neighbors." Cap, jumped out of his chair, followed by Noob and First. Ben hesitated for a couple of seconds got up, and froze.

"Either out there or in here, you're gonna have to face them." Threw back First, rushing out. Ben, a deep sigh escaping his lips, rushed after them.

There was no cover for the advancing aliens once they were beyond the empty and burning ruins of their vehicles. The expanse of white sand in front of them was a killing field. Nonetheless, the aliens advanced.

Cap and Noob took a position on one side of the cave, Ben and First on the other.

They lay down suppressing fire but had to keep taking cover because of the insane intensity of the alien's attack.

"They are going to reach us." Yelled Ben.

"Keep it together, Ben." Noob's voice boomed over the fracas. "We can take them. Just keep them back. We'll be OK." He fired, over and over, scoring a fatal shot every time.

Ben's fire was less effective than Noob's and the aliens shifted accordingly, peppering Noob's position with a vengeance.

The alien line kept coming although they were falling one after the other.

The few standing aliens reach their position and engaged them close up and personal.

One jumped up, bounced on the wall, and came down on Noob, who fired at the last minute, killing his attacker. Another alien approached straight in and, using a wicked-looking bayonet, buried it deep in Noob's abdomen, pushing up towards his chest, piercing his heart and killing him instantly. The alien let out a loud shriek, cut short by a shot from Cap which blew its head clean off.

Ben yelled at them, from an outcropping where he had been sniping at the approaching aliens. "The ones that were retreating are coming back. This is going to get ugly."

Cap ran over to First's position. Their concentrated fire brought down a few more of the attackers.

"We need to take them all out, or we will be overrun." Yelled First.

"Hold this position, I have an idea." He rushed back to Alfa and disappeared through the hatch.

"Where is he going?" Screamed a panicky Ben, "he can't leave now."

"Shut up and shoot." Yelled First.

They were using blasters, which were effective in that any alien they hit, didn't stand back up, but they were using power packs quickly, their reserves dwindling dangerously.

Cap remerged from Alfa with several bundles. Some of the aliens sighted him and started shooting in his direction. First took advantage of the lull in their fire in her direction to snipe a few more.

Cap threw the bundles at the approaching aliens yelling: "Down, take cover." And dived behind a solid outcropping himself.

The ensuing explosions were impressive. The approaching aliens were shredded by the shrapnel propelled forward.

The eerie quiet that followed the last explosion made First neck hairs stand on end. Nothing was moving.

"I think we are done. That's the last of them. It's all over but the cleanup. What did you hit them with?" First asked rushing to Noob's body.

"I used some mining charges we had leftover from our previous trip, I taped them with all the boxes of nuts and bolts we had on hand and hoped for the best." Cap walked slowly, panting, his head on a swivel, scanning for more threats.

"Well, it worked, you can't argue with success."

They stopped and knelt by Noob.

First turned him over gently. Checked for a pulse, but there was nothing. The ugly ragged gash in his abdomen left little doubt he was dead the moment it penetrated his diaphragm. Tenderly, she closed his sightless eyes and stood up.

"He's done. There's no way we could have saved him, even if we could have gotten to him when he went down." Cap put a hand on her back, gently propelling her forward. His attention was on her and their surroundings.

First eyes brimmed over with tears. "I know. It's not fair, though."

Cap stepped back and placed his carabine barrel down on the floor, crossing his hands on the stock and leaning forward a little to rest, and looked up to where Ben was perched. "Hey, Ben. It's all over. Come on down."

Ben didn't move.

First ran and Cap limped over to his elevated position and reached up to him. They pulled him down and he rolled lifeless onto their arms. The far half of his head was blown off by the enemy fire.

"I'm sorry you died in this God-forsaken place. I truly am." Whispered First.

"We have to get a move on." Cap sympathetically put a hand on her shoulder.

"I think we can take a minute. We got all of them, even the rear guard. I don't hear anything from the back, 2812 must have taken them out."

"Unless there are more of them down in that cave. We have to get out of here. On the double. Well, more like you have to get out of here. I'm afraid I'm done." Cap removed his hand from his abdomen. The shirt was heavily stained with blood. The shimmering crimson blotch grew as she watched.

First jumped up and caught Cap as he passed out and started to collapse. She dragged him into Alfa and put him in the medical bay, cleaned the wound, and stapled the deep gash as best she could. After putting an IV in his arm, she administered antibiotics and wound regeneration meds.

Satisfied that was all she could do for Cap, she retrieved Noob's and Ben's bodies, she went up and looked around from the top of the cave, making sure the threat was indeed neutralized. She retrieved what was left of 2812.

She got back to Alfa as quickly as she could, thinking she needed to talk to Gears in the *Einstein's Shadow*.

She was alone. And she was scared.

Chapter 24

"Gears, I'm in a bad way over here, I think I have Alfa repaired enough that we can try to make it up."

"The action looked bad, how's everybody?"

First paused and closed her eyes tight before answering, lowering her head. "Noob is dead." She whispered.

"Damn." Gears' comment was soft, but she heard him over the open comm.

"Ben got killed too."

"Yeah, well, not to be insensitive, but him I didn't know, so, it's sad and all, but as I said, I didn't know him. Where's Cap?" there was a little trembling in Gears' rough voice.

"Badly wounded in the med bay. He is going to survive, but he's out of the fight, for now."

"I guess this is as good a time as any to try and make it out. If the aliens are licking their wounds, you may be able to sneak out of there."

"That's what I thought." She said, her hands going over the preflight procedures.

"We'll be watching. I hate this, not being able to help."

"Thanks but it's the hand I was dealt. I'm taking off now, wish me luck."

She activated the engines and piloted Alfa out of the cave. Careful not to bang the sides, the debris from the battle cascading over the sides. Rocks, loose sand, some of the detritus obscuring her view. Her hands tightened on the controls, aware that right now she was very vulnerable.

Dust and sand flew everywhere as she made her way completely out of the cave. The periphery defense equipment, most of the emplacements were destroyed anyway, would have to stay behind. She didn't want to spend the time picking any up. She needed to leave as soon as possible, the tight opportunity window closing rapidly.

Alfa gained altitude. Piloting by herself was very hard, she had to keep her eyes on sensors and the recently repaired engines. Controlling the bearly working shuttle when it fought her every step of the way was doable but difficult.

"I think I might actually make it this time." A slow shy smile broke out on her lips as she murmured to herself.

The blaring alarm interrupted her thoughts.

An incoming missile. Just the one, but one was enough.

Her evasive maneuvers were countered turn by turn by the missile.

It closed in relentlessly.

She evaded, dipped, climbed, and turned, Alfa fighting her at every maneuver, all to no avail.

Alfa was hit by the concussion from the exploding missile. Not a direct hit, but enough to rattle the ship.

"We saw that." Gears voice from the comm.

"Not right now. A little busy."

She had limited maneuvering control, but she turned to the mound where the missile came from, the top still closing.

"I have something for you, you bastards."

The ammunition for the projectile weapons was completely depleted, but the energy weapons had cooled some and were now available. She brought them online. She sighted the target and made a dive straight for it.

"If I can't pull out of this, you are going to be sorrier than me." Hearing her voice calmed her down a little, she didn't feel quite as alone.

The bolts shot forward with a vengeance, all of them effective. Numerous hits scored on the inside of the closing hatch and blew it open. Her next volley impacted the walls of the hatch and brought them down in a furious rain of rocks, white sand, and dust.

She banked again and tried to gain altitude, but Alfa's damage made it unresponsive.

"I hate this planet. I don't want to die here." Her voice trembled, she knew now she was going to be a very soft target, unable to resist another frontal attack by the aliens.

Activating the landing thrusters, all that's left for her is to select a level, clear area, and land. She hoped the heavily damaged craft made it to a safe landing.

She went down among a huge artificial sand storm caused by Alfa's maneuvering thrusters exerting themselves to avoid a crash.

Finally down, she shut the engines and leaned back, wiping her brow.

She unstrapped, checked sensors to make sure there was no pursuit from the aliens, and rushed to the med bay. Cap was in a bad way, his straps kept him secure, and the med unit was keeping him alive. He had lost a lot of blood and still needed quite a bit more artificial blood to pull him out of unconsciousness. His skin was pale and clammy, his hand cold when she gripped it tight. She supplemented his IV and ran back to the bridge.

She must attack the alien's mound or she'll never be able to leave.

She went to the war chest once more, now almost empty, she had never seen it like this before. Nothing seemed adequate for an attack, just a few weapons, some odds, and ends. Desperate, she ran to the cargo hold. The last time they used Alfa, they were making an asteroid mining run. The miners there had no use for some specific explosives, some mining charges for fracturing asteroids. They didn't need charges to pulverize the material, so they had given them to Cap, to barter or sell at his convenience. They had never gotten around to taking them off Alfa. They were going to come in handy now.

"Gears, I'm going to alien town. Every time we've tried to leave, they shoot us down, time to take the fight to them."

"Are you insane? What are you going to be able to do against all of them? That's it. We are coming down!"

"No, you are not. You will not endanger the ship. You will not leave it unattended either."

"Second can stay here, and I'll—"

"No, you will not. That's not a suggestion or a comment. I'm giving you an order. The two of you can man the ship. It'll be very difficult, but you can, I trust you. If I don't make it, you have to leave us here and make your way to Mobula 3. You have to let them know about this trap."

"Yes. OK. I don't like any of this. But OK"

She went back to the hold, checked on 2812, and after some tweaks, got the robot operational again. The unit was now in even worse shape than before.

"How are you holding up?" She asked 2812 when the diagnostic routines were completed.

"My cores are intact. My body will need to be replaced. I'm down to one effective manipulator again. I will need to interface with the ship's computer to be effective in any way."

"Can you do that? Interface with the computer?"

"Oh, yes, my model is fully flight-capable. Or rather we were at the time of our incident. There might have been some developments that would make the software incompatible or the hardware inaccessible, but I doubt it. My model was way ahead of its time."

A tired smile peeked at First's lips. "You are very modest."

"Not at all, I'm factual at all times."

She could swear that, if it could, the robot would have blushed. She realized she had a soft spot for the circuit salad, even if they only had been together for a short time.

“Be that as it may, let’s see if you can indeed man the guns in your condition. Energy only, I’m afraid, all ammo is spent.”

“To be expected. Human gunners use up a lot more ammo than automated ones, but that is an unavoidable circumstance on a ship like this, I would conclude.”

First shook her head. The soft spot got smaller. “Come on, let’s get this done. I have a date.”

2812 managed to interface and was effective in handling Alfa’s different defensive functions, as well as several of its automated hatches and machinery.

“Keep an eye on Cap.”

“I am. Even now, through internal sensors. It’s a priority to keep the Colonel alive. Shame I was up top when your position was overrun down here, I might have been able to prevent his injuries.”

First turned to 2812 and put her fists on her hips. “Listen, there was nothing you could have done that we didn’t do. Cap is our Captain, I don’t know about this Colonel stuff, but he is our leader. He’s our friend. More of a family than most of us ever had. We did everything in our power. Everything. Noob died, you insensitive bucket of bolts.”

The silence that followed was only broken by First’s agitated breathing.

“You are right, of course. I shouldn’t have said anything.”

First harrumphed and turned around. “Just keep Alfa safe. I’ll be back as soon as I can. If I don’t make it, I’ve ordered Gears to leave, so you’ll be on your own. Take care of Cap.”

She turned around, armed herself, and was walking fast to the hatch when it hit her. The robot had not apologized or admitted to making a mistake. It stated a belief it shouldn't have said anything, not that it was wrong. She had a mind to turn around and let it have a piece of her mind, but there were more important things to do. She realized that she was just looking for excuses not to go and face the aliens again.

She left 2812 on the ship and went to take care of the alien's mound. She took the rivers and streams to mask her heat signature and to take advantage of whatever cover the banks afford her.

As she approached the alien's lair, she decided. She'd end this ... or die trying.

2812 WAS MONITORING THE sensors and making what repairs it could, hindered by having only one operational manipulator.

The blaring alarm was redundant, 2812 had a direct feed from the sensors. The approaching aliens' advance was too swift for 2812 to do much. Rushing back to the bridge, as much as it could in its present condition, it opted to remotely lay down suppressing fire, the only thing available without being physically at the controls.

The alien's brutal frontal attack was intense, but the volume of fire was, in fact, small. 2812 successfully repelled the attack, half of the attacking aliens were laying on the ground, dead, or at least unmoving. The rest retreated in a dense cloud of smoke and dust from their vehicles.

At that precise moment, a claxon went off. They breached the cargo hatch.

2812 rushed back, but in its present condition, any progress was terribly slow. By the time he finally engaged the aliens, they were already making their way through the ship.

Unfamiliar with the layout, they had split into several groups.

The group that chose to go towards the bridge ran headlong into a very effective 2812. It successfully took out their vanguard. Concentrated intense fire with a blaster hit the aliens before they got a shot off.

The rest beat a hasty retreat through the corridors of the ship. 2812 followed them, laying down as much fire as he could all the way to the outer hatch. Every time 2812 went by a fallen alien, he spared the foe on the ground a shot, it did not want any enemies getting up behind him.

All through the engagement, 2812 considered this may all be a distraction and while it was pursuing them, another group might be at the med bay. Taking the Colonel.

Finally, the few surviving enemies were off the ship. 2812 then rushed back as fast as his barely functioning tracks would carry it to check on Cap. The med bay, still with very soft lighting and the constant blinking of the status monitoring devices, lay unperturbed. The aliens had not made it this far.

2812 went back, collecting the bodies littered along the ship's corridors.

It stacked them in the cargo bay for disposal. When it brought in the last one and opened the hatch to push them out of the ship, realized that the area where both Noob's and Ben's bodies were in body bags was in disarray. Ben's body was gone. The aliens took it.

FIRST USED THE SENSOR blocking equipment. Cap trained her to use many of the gadgets and weapons on board. She had always thought the exercises were fun but unnecessary. Now she knew better. She planted the charges on all the access to the alien's compound she could identify. The task took hours, and although the planet, in general, was not warm, she had been at it for a long time, having to climb and crawl, to plant the explosives in crevices and crannies. She was exhausted.

She retreated using the river banks to shield her from view. She had covered all the hatches she had been able to detect. A good thing, since she literally ran out of charges.

She paused, resting against the back of wet compact sand. She was panting and sweating. Her ragged breath came as visible white puffs in front of her face. She cupped some water in her hands and drank deeply of the cool, clear liquid. She wiped her lips with the back of her hand and looked around.

The wind was blowing and some of the fine sand obscured her view. Aside from the whispering of the wind, all was eerily quiet.

She took out the detonator.

You bastards, you are going to hurt. She thought as she removed the security cover.

A sharp pain went through her left leg and she dropped the detonator. She hopped over to the other side as five more impacts hit the bank she was leaning against.

Rolling over, she drew her blaster and sighted over the lip. Six aliens in their silver/white suits were advancing on her position. She took a quick bead on them and squeezed her trigger three times in rapid succession. Three aliens fell, stayed down, unmoving. The other three dived for whatever cover they could find behind mounds or dunes.

Panting hard, she reached down and the hole in her thigh painted her fingers a sticky crimson. She took her belt off and tied it over the wound, pulling tight. A soft whimper escaped her lips, but the aliens already knew where she was.

She rolled over three times and took a quick peek at the last position of the aliens, immediately ducking back down. Three shots kicked up sand as she rolled over to her previous position, popped up, and fired two shots before ducking back down.

She saw one go down but was not sure about the other one.

Over the hissing of the windblown sand, a quiet shuffle reached her.

She rolled over once more and sighted over the top of the embankment. She shot the first alien before it could bring its weapon to bear, but the second one wasted no time and let loose with its gun. A massive blow to her left arm knocked her over. Her second shot went wild, but she corrected her aim before the alien could react and hit it. It staggered back, not a clean hit, but that was all the time she needed. She shot again and this time the alien went down for good.

Bleeding, she searched frantically around. Finally, she moved over a short distance, every move agony, and grabbed the detonator from where she had dropped it.

"A little gift. I hope to hell it's a parting gift, you dirty cannibals."

With a press of the button, she blew the charges. A spectacular series of explosions threw rocks, sand, and debris high in the air and all over. The mound was heavily damaged and now all access she knew of or could see from here were under tons of rocks. A cave-in followed, the thunderous noise accompanied by a huge cloud of white sand and dust going up in the air. She took it as a sure sign the integrity of the alien cave had been compromised. Essentially, they were blocked off. She hoped.

The pain made every move an agony, but she started back, gritting her teeth and hoping that was the end of the alien surprises.

Chapter 25

First's eyes left the ground for a second, it was a struggle to lift her head. Sugar white cold dunes as far as she could see.

Her leg dragged behind her, leaving a shallow furrow on the blood-stained sand. She stumbled forward. Her wounded arm was a dead weight by her side. It didn't even hurt anymore, simply a useless heavy limb hanging from her shoulder. She plowed on.

A shadow fell on her and she lifted her head in time not to bang it against Alfa's side. She held on to the hull as she walked in short faltering steps towards the hatch.

"First, here, let me assist you." 2812 got under her hurt arm and took on some of her weight.

"Good to be back. Didn't get you anything, though, the gift shop sucked."

"You are clearly delirious, we must get you inside."

What started as a chuckle ended in a groan. "A sense of humor. That's one of the first things we gotta buy for you on our next port of call."

It maneuvered her towards the med bay.

She lifted her head and looked around.

"No. We go to the bridge. Now."

"You are badly hurt, you need medical attention."

"I need to get off this mudball, that's what I need. To the bridge, now." She responded through grinding teeth.

2812 started moving in the direction of the bridge. "I must take care of your wounds. I must stop the bleeding."

"No argument from me, but we take off first."

They made it to the bridge.

First fell on the pilot station and started preflight, 2812 rushed as fast as it could out of the bridge.

"Whatever," First said, shaking her head. "Gears, you there?"

"Yes! We saw the fireworks, there is no pursuit, you got clean away."

"Not clean, but yes, I did. I'm preflight right now, I should be airborne in a few."

"The sooner the better."

2812 rolled back onto the bridge, precariously carrying a basket with medical supplies.

"You must allow me to close your wounds before we take off. It would be disastrous if you lost consciousness in flight."

"Yes, mother." First eyes closed and her head fell forward.

"Delirious, again. If I had at least a couple of able manipulators I'd be able to do something more. This is beyond frustrating. You are an irritating human being and tend to treat me as machinery, but on the other hand, you did rescue me from the pile of scrap my logic matrix and cores were tossed in so, I feel I owe you."

First eyes remained closed, as she allowed 2812 to clumsily minister to her wounded arm and leg, which were now hurting. A lot. A smile pulled at her lips. She was conscious, but she could feel the curtains closing on her. She needed to get going, soon, or she would pass out and miss the chance. Perhaps their last chance. "So, you love me? Or what?"

"I do not have the correct sensors to monitor your status adequately, so I had to keep talking to determine when you regained consciousness. Good to have you back, First."

Eyes still closed. "You like me. You think I'm a good person. You may even love me." She giggled.

"You may have a concussion. Definitely, grave wounds that cause delirium, certainly."

"I wish you had a face that could blush, 'cus you'd be purple by now, my friend." A weak smile. "Let's blow this popsicle stand."

She made sure everything was ready and got up. A wave of nausea and disorientation hit her hard.

"Help me, I need to check on Cap, make sure we can take off without hurting him." As they walked haltingly down the different corridors many bloodstains splattered on the floor and walls.

"Anything you've forgotten to tell me?" she asked, nodding towards the maroon splotches visible everywhere.

"There was a quick but rather intense action inside the ship. I was able to neutralize the threat."

A chill went through First. "Cap? Did they reach Cap? Is he alright?"

"No, they did not make it that far. I was able to repel borders before they made it to the med bay." A small pause made her turn to the robot. "I'm afraid they took Ben's body. I do not know why or even when. Sometime during the attack."

"Well, that's not creepy at all," First said with a frown.

After checking on Cap, she got the ship as ready as possible.

"Gears, we are going up. Keep an eye out, if they shoot at us, I'm landing, I can't evade and I don't have any fight left in me."

"Copy, First. Come on over."

2812 called from the weapons station. "I'm ready too. We have all the energy weapons fully charged and online. Any time."

They took off, sand billowing everywhere.

"Anything on sensors?" First was now concentrating on flying Alpha, leaving 2812 to work sensors and weapons.

"No, nothing. There seems to be no activity from alien town. They are closed off, no signals of any sort."

"Keep scanning. I don't want any surprises." First hurt all over, she felt faint but knew this was their last chance. Now or never. "Anything?"

"No. No movement, no heat signatures. Certainly, no new hatches opening up."

First heart was pounding in her chest, as the altimeter informed her that they were gaining altitude. Alpha shook and bucked, it was normally much quicker and smoother than this, but she was happy to be putting distance between herself and the aliens, even if not at the best speed.

The minutes trickled by, almost reluctantly.

The sky above gradually got dark and finally, the welcomed blackness of space engulfed them in orbit.

They made it beyond the atmosphere without incidents.

Chapter 26

"First, you are moving like an arthritic turtle." Gears' rough voice was dripping with concern. "We are coming to pick you up."

"No. Do not move starward. Stay in your current orbit." She winced, careful not to make a sound and have Gears insist on coming to collect them.

"Your shuttle is damaged. You are making lousy time. We can come closer to you and–"

"No. You will hold your position. If you detect any ships coming after us, any ships coming at you from anywhere, in or out system, you will leave immediately. We can always land again and keep resisting as long as we need if we know help is coming. If the *Einstein's Shadow* gets compromised, we are all dead. And on the menu. You do not want that. I don't want that. And since I'm in command, you will follow my orders."

Gears gritted his teeth. "You are the boss."

"I am. So now let me pilot this crate. It's flying with all the grace of a thrown brick."

The trip was tedious and exasperating. The shuttle performed slow, not at its best.

2812 was on sensors with proper machine-like intensity, but there were no further signs from the aliens. No movement, no new secret hatches opening. Nothing.

After several hours, they made it back. First, exhausted, let them hook her up to an IV while Second checked her wounds and administered several medications. Gears took care of Cap, who was still out, but stable, and they moved him to the more complete medical bay of the rig.

"Gears, let's get the *Einstein's Shadow* going. Let's get back underway."

"First, I know you are the boss right now, but we need to fix you up. It will all go a lot better with the three of us working rather than just Second and me. It will take a couple of hours but it'll be worth the time."

She looked like she was going to resist, but her shoulders slumped and she let out all the air in her lungs. There had been nothing from the planet, no movement, nothing. "OK, we'll do it your way. As soon as I'm in a little better shape, we are out of this system."

"Yes, Sir." Said gear with a smile.

First eyes closed and she was out.

SHE WOKE UP AND HER arm was very stiff. The immobilizing gel covers from the wrist to the mid-upper arm, but the wound meds were working on her. She could almost feel the tissues knitting together. Her leg was a different matter. The immobilizing gel was from her ankle all the way to her hip, she couldn't flex her knee. Below the belt, the sensation was very different. Her leg hurt. A lot. That meant she probably had an infection besides the physical damage.

Oh well, if it hurts, it means the leg wouldn't have to come off, so that's good. I hope.

She got up, groaning. She took in the med bay, the lights were subdued, she imagined it was Gears' way to keep her sleeping a little longer. She moved over to where Cap was. His readings were all stable, on the lower edge of normal, but probably out of danger. He was still out. A good thing, she thought, she needed him to be wide awake and ready for command when he came to. She headed to the bridge, gritting her teeth with each step. Her immobilized leg made her limp all the way.

"Is the buoy still transmitting?" she asked as she walked on the ample bridge of the *Einstein's Shadow*.

"Yes, loud and clear." He routs the signal to the bridge speakers, where they can hear it. "It's the salvage signal, so no one should stop for the emergency signal. We read it steadily since–"

Right at that moment, the signal died.

"Damn. They were not all out of the fight after all, and they made their way out of their spider hole."

"The only signal coming out now is the emergency signal. It is ..." Second checked the receiver. "Gone. The signal is gone too."

A chill went down First's spine. "Keep an eye on the planet, watch for any departures. They had the capabilities to take down a ship in orbit at some point. They have not done anything to indicate they can reach us here, but better safe than sorry. Let's get ready to clear this system, I want us in FTL ASAP."

She settled in the sensor station, the calculations made, checked, and rechecked by Second, Gears, and the computer several times while the landing party was on the planet.

At sensors and manning weapons, First kept a wary eye on the planet, ready to react instantly if they detected a ship's departure or any aggression from the planet.

No ships came after them, no missile fired, and soon they made it to interstellar space.

"Ready to engage." Called out Second.

"Go to FTL." Ordered First from the sensor station, keeping an eye on the system they were leaving behind, expecting a nasty surprise at any second.

"In the pipe." Called out Second. He smiled. "Estimated arrival time is just a week late, we might even make up some time in system at destination." And he sat back.

First's shoulders eased a little and she realizes that, for the first time since going down to the planet, she was safe and could truly relax.

Chapter 27

First and Gears took their time and reassembled 2812 into an effective combat robot thanks to some parts and pieces in the hold of the ship. Cap's resources still surprised everyone.

First was finishing up the refitting of 2812, putting the final touches, and removing any stains or smudges on the matte black new body, while Gears went to relieve Second. He now looked like a utility robot but was an intelligence-gathering battle 'bot underneath.

"I finally have adequate equipment. It feels marvelous to be whole again. Fortunately, the Colonel had this equipment on board."

"I don't think luck had anything to do with it, I think there's more to Cap than meets the eye, and I've known him for a lot of years. And, by the way, I thought you had changed his denomination to Cap, no?"

"I should refer to the Colonel as Colonel when no one but the crew is around, proper military decorum. You have traveled with him for a lot of years, as you say, you probably don't really know him. Only someone like myself could possibly know him."

First laughed out loud at the robot. "OK, Sass, I'll take your word for it."

"Sass? Are you addressing me?"

"Yes. I am."

"That's not my denomination."

If First didn't know better, she'd swear the robot was offended.

"Listen, it's my pet name for you. Sass."

"Pet name? So you consider me a pet?"

First again laughed, "Oh, my, no, I don't consider you a pet."

"So, you consider yourself my pet."

"Hey. Listen, buddy ..." First took a deep calming breath before continuing. "We all have special names, mine is First, it doesn't mean anyone is anyone's pet. It's just a manner of speaking."

"Sass. OK, I'll allow it."

First rolls her eyes and threw the rag she had in her hands at the robot's head, which it catches in the air. "Let's go to the bridge, Sass."

AFTER TWO DAYS IN THE pipe Cap woke up, hungry and curious as to how it all ended. He had something to eat and walked on the bridge just a few moments ahead of First and Sass.

"Here we are." She announced as she entered the bridge, with Sass right behind her. "Meet Sass, the new member of the crew." A statement received with chuckles from everyone. "I still can't believe you had all this ... junk in the ship."

"I was trained to be a pack-rat," Cap explained shrugging. He was pensive for quite a while. They probably did not expect him to go on. Sighing deeply, he decided to take them fully in his confidence. "Waste not, want not. Truth is, I was military intelligence, and when they cashiered me, I was given the option of keeping this ship. I was going to get one just like it anyway. It was adapted to pass as a hauler, that was our cover, my team and me, to be stellar haulers. The ship was fully military equipped, though, so I had them leave all the goodies and ... well, what can I say? I like toys. I buy them when I have access to them." A smile of pride shone on his face, as he tenderly stroked the helm.

"What about you Sass? Do we have to return you to your unit or something?" Asked First.

"This is my unit. As I stated before, I had a full dossier with the viable officers that could take over command. Once I was reactivated, I had to find an officer to be my superior and controller."

"And I reactivated you." First leans forward, putting her elbow on the console and her chin on her fist.

"You did. You, however, were not in the chain of command at the time. The Colonel was. He was automatically registered as my new commanding officer. That means I now fit in the command structure here and can properly obey lawful orders from the ship's complement. Since by the Colonel's presentation, his tasks deal with intelligence, I will blend and pretend to be nothing more than a galactic hauler service robot. Until otherwise instructed by the Colonel or by any of you."

They all looked at each other.

"Uh, Cap?" First asked intrigued. "Are we supposed to hand him back?"

Sass turned to Cap as if interested in the answer.

"I had time to ponder on that very question while I was laid up. No, we don't. He is legitimately part of the crew. He has been written off by now since the transport never made it to its destination. If we turned him back, he'd most likely be decommissioned, given the time he has been off-grid, he could not be integrated into a unit due to the risk of his program having been corrupted, and reprograming him completely wouldn't be cost-effective. So we keep him. Legitimate salvage."

"Cap ... him? He?"

"Yes, Second, we can't keep calling him it." Cap turned to Sass. "Unless you prefer to be a she?"

"My speaker is modulated for a male voice, so *he* is acceptable. Should I change my denomination officially to Sass?" First could swear he was pleading against it, so she had to work hard not to laugh out loud.

"Yes. Do so. And, please, address me as Cap at all times. I know you would not make the mistake of calling me Colonel in public, but, if you always call me Cap, there's no risk of being overheard even by accident. And also, intelligence, remember?" A smile danced on Cap's lips.

"Acknowledged, Cap."

"Great." Cap chuckled softly.

MOBULA 3 GREW IN THE monitor as they approached the planet.

"Mobula 3 control, this is the *Einstein's Shadow*, with general cargo."

"*Einstein's Shadow*, Mobula 3. Welcome, you guys are a couple of days late. What happened?"

"Long story, I'm afraid. We will need Colonial Authority officers at the debriefing. We have some stories to tell them."

The story about the cannibalistic aliens was shocking all around, at first received with utter and overt disbelief.

The recordings of the alien's lair, the recordings of some of the engagements, of Ben's story, and certainly all the sensor data eventually convinced even the most skeptic of the lot. The recovered jewelry and some other things and readings they managed to get from the wreck were further proof. Given the multiple pieces of evidence they presented, a heavily armed military patrol was sent to check.

They were paid for their cargo and transport. Also, the bonuses from Stellar Cartography for the recordings of the unknown system and a little something for the location of the wreck for salvage. The salvage itself would be carried out by people from Mobula 3, after the aliens had been taken care of. They presented enough jewelry to make their case but kept some and all the ingots, which would fetch a nice price in the more developed, affluent worlds.

They reported Noob's death, sent his money to the next of kin, and told them he had a space burial.

Turned out Ben was actually the Captain of the ship that took him there. He clearly felt guilty about what had happened and chose to deceive them. However, why the aliens had taken him in the end, remained a mystery.

They recruited a new crewperson. They were lucky enough to find a supernumerary crewperson they already knew from previous trips who was happy to sign up with them as a Noob again.

As they were finishing loading up for the return trip at the end of an uneventful six months, they convened at the galley.

"Cap, you haven't told anyone about Sass. I know we decided to keep him and all, but you didn't even try."

"No. I didn't First. I hope that's not a problem." He smiled at her over his soup.

"Not at all, I've grown attached to the little wind-up toy. And you, old bucket of bolts, have not asked to be returned to your unit."

"I am far from a bucket, although I do have several bolts. My unit perished on that planet. We fought and we were defeated. We were on an intelligence-gathering mission, I was to serve as protection and support to the unit and the local group we were to reinforce. My unit is gone. Your tinkering with my matrix has eliminated some restrictions placed on my personality matrix. I am, as you would say, a free agent now. Since I am a robot, I need to be assigned to a function. You have shown yourselves to be decent human beings, and you are fun to be with. So, I have attached to your group."

"And if we had not met with your approval? What then?"

"Cap probably knows. I would have presented myself to the local governing body and asked to be returned to my theoretically rightful outfit. Probably would have ended up here, lobotomized and doing patrol or guard duties. Most likely completely disassembled for parts. So, this is a better option."

Cap was laughing softly.

"So, do we have a deserter or what?" Insisted First, smiling.

"Not at all. Like he said, his unit was destroyed on that planet. No one is looking for him. His unit is probably deemed lost in space and it will be confirmed when they check the planet out. So there are no strings on him."

"Huh. Who knew?"

Second and Gears popped in. "What's good?"

"Soup's decent. Are we about ready?"

They both served themselves and sat with Cap.

"We'll be ready in about three hours."

Cap pushed his bowl towards the center of the table. "First, how do you feel?"

She turned to look at Cap, a frown on her face. "What do you mean? I'm all better, a couple of more scars, but nothing wrong."

"What do you think about Second here? What's your evaluation of him?"

She looked around evidently a little bewildered. Second looked from one to the other, clearly unsure what to say.

"Very able spaceman, Cap. You know that. He's great."

"Think he is ready to be First? Are you up for it, Julio?"

First's face was a study in conflicting emotions, she looked intrigued, hurt, disoriented.

Second was evidently shocked when Cap used his name rather than his designation. His eyes were wide open like huge saucers. "I'd never take First place, Cap, not unless she was leaving." He turned to First, a new surprised expression working his face. "You are not leaving, are you?"

Cap chuckled a little. "Not if she doesn't want to. I've had feelers out for some time for another rig. You know this, First." She nodded, still with a puzzled expression on her face. "Well, one is available, just like this one, well, a little newer perhaps. I could buy it by myself, but it'd strain my resources. If you decide to come in as my partner, you could captain her."

First sat back in her seat. She shook her head and, after a moment, let out a huge happy laugh.

"And what are we calling my rig, partner?"

"It's got an awful name right now, *Stella Nova* or something. How do you feel about *Alcubierre's Bubble*?"

"Love it."

Maggie, her denomination as First now obsolete, realized this was the start of a fantastic new chapter in her life. She now understood why Cap was still at the helm of his ship after so much time and so many hard knocks. She knew he had been grooming her for her own command. Cap trusted her abilities enough to ask her to partner with him. He had the money to retire, but why retire, when this life was still there to live? She looked forward to her new command.

The little villa of her dreams? Well, she could always have a very small one in her port of origin, for the rare times she was planet-bound between trips.

Life looked better than ever.

THE END

Don't miss out!

Visit the website below and you can sign up to receive emails whenever T.J. Manrique publishes a new book. There's no charge and no obligation.

https://books2read.com/r/B-A-SDFT-OKSZB

BOOKS 2 READ

Connecting independent readers to independent writers.

Did you love *Einstein's Shadow Galactic Hauler*? Then you should read *The Rhea Initiative Project*[1] by T.J. Manrique!

[2]

Earth holds bitter memories. When he looks to the stars for answers, will he rocket to victory or fly too close to the sun?

Bill Barecraft is lost in the depths of grief. With his business success making him a target for extortion, he's devastated when a violent gang kidnaps his wife and children. And when his money can't stop the abductors from brutally executing his family, the heartbroken man channels his despair into an ambitious dream to populate other planets.

---

1. https://books2read.com/u/bw1dNG
2. https://books2read.com/u/bw1dNG

Assembling some of the world's brilliant minds, he tries to heal through the excitement and challenge of conquering interstellar travel. But even as the team edges closer to leaving the solar system, their launch plans get derailed by a ruthless organization intent on destroying all hope.

Will his vision be torn apart by vicious politics, or can they find peace in space?

T.R.I.P. The Rhea Initiative Project is a slow-burn standalone science fiction thriller. If you like damaged heroes, mind-bending ideas, and high-stakes action, then you'll love T.J. Manrique's near-future shot into the galaxy.

Buy T.R.I.P. The Rhea Initiative Project today to begin the countdown!

Read more at https://tjmanrique.com/.

Also by T.J. Manrique

The Rhea Initiative Project
Einstein's Shadow Galactic Hauler
Zombies That's what happened
Another Boring Day In Space

Watch for more at https://tjmanrique.com/.

About the Author

T.J. Manrique always enjoyed reading. His uncle gave him a Jules Verne book at 10, which started of a torrid love affair with the genre. He also enjoyed Ian Fleming and Agatha Christie. He was mesmerized by the B&W TV serials Buck Rogers and Flash Gordon. He found Star Trek in the late 60s. He was in college when Star Wars came out and his professors cemented his passion for the genre by having Sand People and Jawas be the subjects of his genetics midterms. Analyzing the biomechanics of the xenomorphs and humans was a natural progression. He currently lives in Florida with his wife and youngest daughter where he is indulging in his passion for reading and writing.

Read more at https://tjmanrique.com/.

About the Publisher

A small publishing company. Currently starting out in the fields of Science Fiction, Techno Thrillers, Fantasy and Horror.

CPSIA information can be obtained
at www.ICGtesting.com
Printed in the USA
BVHW081144060922
646311BV00005B/219